Kim & Daniel Chamberlain.

Thanks for your support! :)

consequences Linda

When Love Is
Blind

a novella

Linda R. Herman

𝒳𝒴
PUBLISHING

Xpress Yourself Publishing, LLC
P. O. Box 1615
Upper Marlboro, Maryland 20773

ISBN-10: 0-9799757-0-0
ISBN-13: 978-0-9799757-0-7

Library of Congress Control Number: 2007939068

Printed in the United States of America

Cover and Interior Designed by
The Writer's Assistant
www.thewritersassistant.com

Visit Xpress Yourself Publishing on the World Wide Web at:
www.xpressyourselfpublishing.org

For Ollie M. West
Sunrise: February 14, 1941 – Sunset: January 14, 2006

I dedicate this novella, and all of my works, to a woman who dedicated her life to me, my late grandmother Ollie M. West. God called her home on January 14, 2006, but she is always with me. In every thought that crosses my mind and every word that I utter, she is there. I am eternally grateful for having her as my mother, grandmother, and friend for thirty years.

Acknowledgments

First and foremost, I give thanks to God above. Without Him, the gift and love of writing would not dwell within me.

For everyone who has lost a loved one to AIDS and for everyone who struggles with the disease, please know that with God all things are possible. It is truly going to take unity and a lot of faith in God to beat this deadly disease.

There are so many people I owe thanks. If you don't see your name on this list, know that you are in my heart even if you temporarily eluded my thoughts. I give thanks to my family, my grandfather, James D. West. His belief in hard, honest work brings me to this moment. I thank my parents and in-laws Sander West and Johnny Royal, Ronnie and Lorraine Herman and Betty Akins, my siblings, Johnny, Demarcus, Chynethia, Malcolm, Tonya, Tammy, and Fredrick—love you all. Thanks to my aunts and uncles who have always been more like my sisters and brothers, Dorothy, Donna, Oscar, James Jr., Johnny, and Jesse.

I thank my cousin, Shakesta, whom I love as my own child. To all the Royals, Cones, Wests, Corbins, Akins, and Hermans…thank you and I love you all for supporting me.

A very special thanks to my immediate family, for you are the ones who have really stood by me and endured countless sacrifices, my husband, Ronnie, my son, Quantavius, my stepdaughter, Shrelle, and last but not least, my Baby girl, Jordyn. A special thanks as well to my co-workers at Crisp Co 911 for reading for me and being a support system. Laressa Taylor, Tawanna Reese, Melissa Swain, Dechelle Davis, Amber Brown, and the whole crew-thank you and I love you.

I have met so many wonderful authors whom I must thank. Fon James, my very first online pal, Allyson Deese, my baby sister of the pen, Casche Russell, Elissa Gabrielle, Peron F. Long, Melissa Wathington, Kisha Green, Tinisha Nicole Johnson, Brandy Johnson, Wanda Campbell, Ebony Dawn, DL Sparks, Sonya Sparks, Margie Gosa Shivers, Lee Hayes, members of the Writers Rx, The Writers Hut, Lavender Isis Press, Afro-European Sisters Network, Essence of Romance, APOOO, and the list is on going. Thank you all for embracing me. For me this adventure began with a short story submission to Black Expressions. I thank their editor, Carol Mackey immensely! And mad shout outs to all the authors at Xpress Yourself Publishing and ASA, where Authors Support Authors! ASA is a group you should definitely check out on the web at www.freewebs.com/asanetwork.

And finally, I thank Jessica Tilles, founder of Xpress Yourself Publishing. Jessica, thank you for your faith in me, your patience, and your love. From the moment I first blundered into the Writers Rx, you have been one of the most helpful people I have encountered. You are so full of wisdom and insight and so willing to share your knowledge. May God always bless you, Jessica! Thank you so much for taking a chance on this young lady from Cordele, Georgia!

And to the readers, thank you and may God be with you! Visit www.xpressyourselfpublishing.org for all of my future works.

Be blessed and well read!

Linda R. Herman

consequences
When Love Is
Blind

Chapter 1

WITH THE RECEIVER PLASTERED TO my ear, I couldn't believe what Andre was saying to me. It was our seventeenth wedding anniversary and he was calling to tell me he had a late meeting with a client. We wouldn't be able to go out and celebrate as planned. I would have to call and cancel our dinner reservations.

Disappointment rose from deep within, lodging in my throat. "Are you sure you can't reschedule?" I pouted, not wanting to cancel our reservations at Chez La Vous, a popular upscale French restaurant that I had to schedule reservations six months in advance, and here he was telling me that he couldn't make it. I planned for us to enjoy a nice dinner followed by a late night drive, and then an intense night of lovemaking.

"It's the only night he is free, Sade. I'm really sorry, baby. We'll have to celebrate another night." He apologized, yet again.

So angry, and unable to muster a sound above a whisper, I said, "Okay," before he told me again he was sorry and that he loved me. Damn it, I didn't want to hear his apologies. I wanted to hear him tell me we were going to spend our anniversary together, as we're supposed to do, and as we'd done for the last seventeen years.

Placing the phone in its cradle, I solemnly headed upstairs to take off my evening gown. I didn't need it just to sit at home and watch TVLand. George and Weezie didn't care what I was wearing.

"Why tonight?" I asked rhetorically as I dragged myself into my bedroom. I didn't want to celebrate our anniversary some other time. I wanted to celebrate it tonight. We were married on June 15th, not the 16th or 17th. I knew how important his clients were to him but who wouldn't understand a man being with his wife on their anniversary?

Stepping out of black three-inch heels, I unzipped the gown and watched it billow down around my feet. Lazily, I picked it up and hung it in the closet, and sighed heavily. Staring at the dress, once again, disappointment knotted my stomach. I really wanted to show off my new dress. It was black and black is beautiful. It fell just below my knees and I looked great in it. At thirty-five years old, five-six and one-hundred forty-five pounds, I looked damn good. I didn't have the pouch that some mothers couldn't get rid of after having babies. Doing several crunches a day was how I maintained my flat tummy. My breasts were full and my hips and butt were curvy.

Only wearing a red, silk thong and a matching bra, I admired my body in the full-length mirror. "Andre, how can you pass up on this? I was going to put it down tonight," I said as I gave myself a pat on my full, firm bottom. "I know what I can do!" I yelled excitedly.

Taking off the bra and thong, I pulled out a long, black trench coat from the closet, and slipped into it. I stepped back into the black three-inch heels. If Andre couldn't come to me, I would go to him. I was determined to make sure our anniversary was memorable.

With excitement building inside me, I rushed down the stairs to the kitchen and grabbed the basket of wine, strawberries and whipped cream that I prepared for our after dinner treat.

Wearing nothing but a trench coat and heels, I slid behind the wheel of my silver Lexus and drove to Andre's office. "When he sees me in this trench coat, in the middle of June, I'm sure he'll get the hint and end his meeting ASAP!" I said to myself, as I peeled out of the driveway. In all the years of our marriage, we never made love in his office and I was looking forward to blowing his mind.

When I pulled into the parking lot, Andre's black Porsche was the only car visible. I guessed his client hadn't made his first big vehicle purchase yet. Andre represented players in both the NBA and NFL. A lot of them purchased fancy sports cars and big houses before the ink dried on their newly negotiated contracts. I guessed this one was very new and hadn't gotten around to that just yet.

I took the elevator to the fifth floor, to Andre's office. His secretary's desk was empty. I wasn't surprised. Tarilyn normally didn't work late when Andre had after hour's meetings with clients. She normally had all the paperwork prepared prior to five o'clock. Andre often bragged about how great of an assistant she was and had been for the past few years. We both liked her a lot.

I left the basket with the wine and strawberries at her desk. Approaching Andre's office, I noticed that the door was closed. Now, why was the door closed after hours? Standing in front of the door, and just before I knocked, I heard noises that caused me to stop, with my hand in mid-air.

"Is that all you got? Come with it!" an unfamiliar male's voice said.

"Can you handle it? How about that?" Andre teased.

Both sounded out of breath, panting like a couple of dogs in heat. This can't be what it sounded like.

As rage built within me, I didn't knock on the door or even reach for the door handle. Before I knew it, I raised my leg as high as I could and kicked the door wide open! Gasping and covering my mouth, the door bounced off the wall, slowly winding down to a partial closing. The scene before me was horrific. My husband had a young man bent over his desk, with their pants down around their ankles.

My legs weakened. "Oh God! Oh God!" I screamed to the top of my lungs. This had to be a nightmare. My husband wasn't gay. The man I married, the father of my kids, would never touch another man in this way! Never had I suspected him of anything close to what I was seeing. What had I done wrong in my life to deserve this?

Andre quickly withdrew from his lover and pulled up his pants. The young man was so into their disgusting lovemaking that he didn't realize I was there.

Finally, he made eye contact with me and exclaimed, "Oh shit!"

"Sade...," Andre said, walking toward me, fastening his pants.

I raised my hand, stopping him in his tracks. I didn't want him near me! I looked at the young man and yelled, "Get the hell out of here! Get out of here now before I kill your ass!"

He tried to pull his pants up while running toward me, and the door. He fell but never stopped moving, quickly scattering toward the door before rising to his feet. As he passed me, he said, "I'm sorry, Ma'am. I'm so sorry!"

I didn't know who he was or even if he played basketball or football. He probably had a girlfriend who, like me, didn't know he had a boyfriend. He's a pretty young boy of no more than twenty-two, with a light complexion and dark wavy hair. I couldn't tell for sure how tall he was since he was ass up over the desk and then running and falling down.

"I can explain," Andre said, with all the nerve in the world.

Peering at him with a clamped mouth and fixed eyes, I yelled, "What's to explain? I just caught you fucking another man!"

"Lower your voice!" he said in a hushed tone as if it were during business hours.

"Who's going to hear me?" I asked, looking around.

After a few moments of silence, he said, with a heavy sigh, "I'm not gay, Sade. I was just trying something different."

Folding my arms across my chest, I tilted my head to the side. "Not gay?" I asked in disbelief, with a raised brow. "What else is it called when a man fucks another man, Andre?" I anticipated his response. It took every ounce of restraint I had not to pick up the first thing I got my hands on and knock him in his head!

"He's gay!" he said pointing at the empty doorway. His lover, like Elvis, had left the building. I didn't know how he arrived or how he left, but I did know for sure that he was gone. "He's the one who gets turned out. Nobody is going up in me." He patted his wide chest, like Tarzan.

I couldn't believe my ears. Andre was an intelligent man. He couldn't be so naïve that he only defined gay as the man who played the bottom role. I don't care if you're the fucker or the fuckee, when two men had sex, or two women had sex, they are both gay!

I gathered the words to a question I wasn't sure I wanted the answer to. "Is he the first?" I tightened the belt around my trench coat. I felt stupid for driving over there wearing nothing but damn high heels and a trench coat. This night would definitely be memorable but it wouldn't be because I was the one putting it down, that's for sure.

He lowered his eyes and stared blankly at the floor. That's when I realized I'd been living in the dark. He'd been living a double life and, as always, I, the wife, was the last to know.

I sighed deeply. "How long has this been going on?" I'd been so stupid!

"I was curious in high school but I didn't start experimenting until college," he admitted without looking at me, the coward. "It's nothing I do all the time, Sade. Sometimes I just want something different," he had the audacity to proclaim.

I threw my hands up in surrender. "It's different," I sarcastically said as I turned to walk away. That much I couldn't argue. A gay relationship was definitely different.

"What's with the trench coat?" he asked before I exited his office. I stopped abruptly and massaged my temples. I felt a headache coming on, because I couldn't stand the sight of him or the sound of his voice. If I didn't get out of there, I would kill him, even if I had to do it with my bear hands.

I spun around, unloosened the belt and opened the coat wide. I allowed his eyes to roam over my nakedness because his hands never would again.

"This is what you didn't want," I snarled.

"Can we talk about this?" he pleaded as I closed the coat and tightened the belt around my waist.

"We're going to go and get tested for AIDS first thing Monday morning. I don't care what kind of meetings you have. Cancel them," I ordered as I walked out of the office. But, before I took another step, I turned to face him. "Don't even think about coming home tonight unless you want me to cut your dick off and stick it up your ass. Now, that's something different!"

"I'm not gay!" he continued to yell as he followed on my heels. I stepped inside the elevator. "Don't say anything about this, please!" he begged as the elevator doors closed.

The tears threatened to fall but I couldn't give into the pain, not yet. Whom would I want to tell? I'm a beautiful woman who caught her husband fucking another man. What did that say about me? Was this my fault? Was I not woman enough for him?

As I'm walking off the elevator, the fuckee was in the lobby, sitting in a chair, looking pitiful. He jumped up to run toward the door when he heard the click-clack of my heels.

"No need to fear. If that ten-inch dick didn't hurt you, neither can I." I pulled my keys out of my pocket. "You may as well go back up there and finish up. He's not coming home with me."

"I'm sorry about everything, Ma'am. I really am," he said with a thick Latino accent. He looked black, mixed with Puerto Rican. Even in my anger, I couldn't deny that he was very attractive. Like Andre, he exhibited no signs of being gay. Then again, what were the signs of begin gay? Did I even know?

I wasn't mad at the young man. He's not the man I married seventeen years ago. He didn't father my kids. I didn't lie beside him every night never suspecting that he was gay. No, I wasn't mad at him at all. Actually, I pitied him because he was one more black man who was too afraid to accept and admit to his sexuality. He was one more black man who would marry and father kids but would always have that taste for *something different*. Every now and then, he would be a fucker or a fuckee but never admit that he was gay.

"Good night," I said to him, as the look in my eyes expressed the sadness in my heart. I was sad for both of us.

I left, not caring if he returned to Andre's office or not. I didn't care what they did to each other. I hated what Andre had done to our marriage. How was I going to explain this to our children, family and friends? Everyone thought we were so in love; I thought it too. I really was in love. For seventeen years, we lived a fairytale life. Everything was perfect until Andre went and fucked it up with a nasty, unhappy ending.

I loved him but I couldn't stay married to him. I couldn't pretend like my eyes played tricks on me. Through amber-colored eyes, I saw my husband having sex with another man. I would be a fool to put myself at risk by staying with him. It was shame on him when I didn't know. Now that I knew, it was shame on me.

In my mind, the disgusting scene played over and over, ugly images of my husband loving another man. And, the smell of two men that permeated the air made me sick to my stomach. "God, please let the results be negative," I silently prayed as I pulled into my driveway, determined the next step would be to the clinic.

It was hard enough to swallow the fact that my marriage was over but the worse case scenario would be receiving positive results. It's a death sentence and there's no undoing it. How dare he determine my fate? Who did he think he was, God?

When I made my way upstairs, I fell on my bed and cried myself to sleep as darkness blanketed the room. This was not how I planned this evening.

Chapter 2

EARLY MONDAY MORNING, ANDRE AND I were at the clinic to take our tests. Over the weekend, his attempts to reach out to me went unanswered. I refused to talk to him during the test as well.

"Have you been exposed to the disease?" the nurse asked.

I told her yes and rolled my eyes at Andre.

He said nothing.

He tried to get me to talk to him in the parking lot, but I refused. When I arrived home, there was a message on the machine. It was Andre reminding me that the kids would be coming home in a few weeks and he didn't want them to think we were not together. I laughed at the message because we were *not* together. As far as I was concerned, we would never *be* together.

I hadn't told the kids or anyone about our separation, or the reason behind it. The kids were spending the summer with my parents down south in Cordele, Georgia. They traveled all over the world with Andre and me on family vacations but nothing was more fun to them than helping my dad with watermelons in the Watermelon Capital of the World.

When they asked about their father, I would tell them he was working late and that they could reach him on his cell phone. I was sure he wouldn't tell them what was really going on. He was too ashamed and in denial. Let him tell it, he wasn't gay despite the fact that I caught him in the act. What worried me most, though, was that when he withdrew from his lover, he wasn't wearing a condom.

I'd never thought about the possibility of being infected with AIDS before. I hadn't been with anyone other than Andre. I thought we were in a monogamous relationship. Well, I was but obviously, my husband wasn't. I thought I would feel less afraid had I caught him with another woman. I knew it was still dangerous but for him to have unprotected sex with a man really concerned me. He'd been living this double life for a long time. It was highly possible that we had been infected at some point.

Standing before the bathroom mirror, I peered at my reflection, looking for anything different. I looked the same. I felt fine. But, I'm too smart to think that meant I couldn't have AIDS. The seventy-two-hour waiting period was really scaring me.

♋ ♋ ♋ ♋ ♋

When I met my literary agent for lunch on day two, she noticed how nervous I was. Cindy Brown and I were friends and had worked together for several years. I'm a novelist and she was there by my side when I wrote my first novel. Now that I had completed my ninth novel, we were celebrating by having lunch.

"Is everything okay? You seem a little anxious." She nodded toward my full plate of spinach and romaine. "You've hardly touched your salad."

I stopped playing in the dish, laid the fork to the side and sighed. "I just miss my kids. When they come back home they'll be juniors. Soon, they'll be leaving home for a lot longer than just summer. They'll be leaving home for good." It wasn't the whole truth but it wasn't totally a lie.

"You better hope so!" Cindy teased. When she realized I wasn't laughing with her, she placed her hand over mine and apologized. "I was trying to make you feel better. I can only wish my lazy son wouldn't have returned home after college."

"What has Brandon been up to?" I asked as I pictured Cindy's only son. With an athletic build, he was very clumsy. He was smart with a degree in criminal justice, and could be anything he wanted to be but he lacked ambition.

"Up? He hasn't been up off my couch in months," Cindy said as she rolled her eyes, taking a sip of her wine.

"I need to call Judge Mathis and get some advice about tough love. That child has to get out of my house. Stan and I need our privacy."

Stan was Cindy's new boyfriend. He was ten years her senior and he loved her. I think she finally found the right man. She deserved it. She was very lonely when her husband, Roger, ran off with his much younger secretary five years ago.

In her mid-forties and stunning, Cindy was a tall woman, about six feet, with a toned body, and a pretty face. She resembled Cindy Crawford, only she was naturally blonde. Even though she was a white female, she was curvaceous like the sisters. Her new love, Stan, was a brother. They were happy and I was happy for them.

"I hear ya!" I told her, trying to pep up.

"How's Andre?" she asked, not knowing that she just killed my pep.

"He's the same ol' same ol'. You know Andre." I picked up the dessert menu. I needed something to put in front of my face to hide my sour expression. The last thing I wanted to talk about was Andre.

Her cell phone rang. I could tell by her sultry voice that it was Stan. When she said goodbye to him she told me she was sorry to run, but Stan wanted her to meet him at his office. He was a pediatrician.

I told her I understood and we kissed cheeks. She congratulated me on how well my novel was doing and encouraged me to go for number ten. Then she was gone. I stayed a while longer and finished my drink.

I thought about the characters in my latest novel. The wife found out her husband had a five-year-old child with another woman, who was determined to be the next Mrs. and she would stop at nothing to break the couple up. I thought they had problems when I created them but I would trade my real life for a fiction one any day. At the end of the novel, the husband and wife lived happily ever after with all of the kids and the other woman was killed by an ex-boyfriend with a grudge.

When I arrived home, I could tell that Andre was here. He left flowers with a card that I didn't read. I threw all that mess in the trash. He had better be glad he left before I got home. I still wanted to castrate his ass. Some soon-to-be dead flowers and a sentimental card weren't going to erase what I saw.

I felt waves of nausea at the thought of the scene. I lie down and try not to think about Andre and his young male lover. I only prayed that homosexuality or bi-sexuality was not something that was passed down in family genes. I didn't want my son, AJ, Andre Junior, growing up to be sexually confused like his father. I never wanted him to hurt a person the way his senior had hurt me.

Even though it was only seven o'clock, I decided to take a long bubble bath and then go straight to bed. I didn't have the strength to do anything more. Life was taking such a toll on me that I didn't even remember my head hitting the pillow before I succumbed to sleep. Imagine my surprise when I woke up a few hours later and discovered Andre lying next to me. I hadn't heard him enter the room.

He had some nerve! After witnessing him with another man, he had to be crazy to think I would welcome him into my bed, ever again. I did to him what I should have done the night I caught him with his male lover. I slapped him so hard; he sat straight up in the bed. "What the hell are you doing here?"

Stunned, he rubbed his left cheek. "I live here, too! You can't put me out of my own house, Sade. I gave you some time to cool off."

"Get out!" I yelled as I picked up the lamp from the nightstand and threatened to bash him in his head.

Jumping out of bed, he yelled, "I bought this damn house! I'm not going anywhere! You can take the little money you've made writing your stupid books and leave!"

Knowing he wasn't supportive of my writing, this confirmed it. I longed for encouraging words that rarely came. When the kids were small, he wouldn't watch them for me when I worked to meet deadlines. I had to do the best I could, managing family and career.

I didn't work outside of the house after college because, despite my degree in journalism, Andre wanted me at home. The kids were in school and he was at work but he wanted me to be accessible in case they needed me during the day. Therefore, he felt it best that I didn't commit to a job. I agreed and took freelance assignments. Then one day when I was bored, I started writing and before long, I had a novel.

"I don't mind leaving," I declared, as I headed to the closet. He could have his damn house. I would gladly get my shit and go! If I stayed here, I would end up being cellmates with a big bitch named Bertha.

"I'm sorry, Sade. I don't want you to leave." He hurried toward me, and if looks could kill… he stopped in his tracks. He knew not to come any closer. "I'll go sleep in the guest room. I won't bother you." He took one of his suits and a few accessories out of the closet and solemnly dragged his feet down the hall to the guest suite.

Locking the bedroom door behind him, I waited about an hour before I fell off to sleep. I wanted to make sure he didn't try to sneak back in. We were to get our test results tomorrow and I didn't want to be arrested tonight. I was not ready to be cell buddies with Big Bertha.

The alarm sounded at seven. I dragged myself out of bed and into the shower. I dressed casually in a long blue jean dress and sandals. My hair was still pinned up. My stylist did it for me Friday morning since I was anticipating a romantic evening with my husband on our anniversary. Our last anniversary.

My stylist, Amber, was actually someone I grew up with in Cordele. She and her husband, Kareem, who was a barber, moved to Atlanta a few months ago. I was so glad to hear from her when she called to tell me she was in town. I gave her name and information to a lot of the big wigs in the community to build up her clientele. It worked. Both she and Kareem got a lot of business. They worked in the same building: she up front and he in the back. She said it reminded her of her sister- and brother-in–law's set up at home. Sandi and Wayne were in a duplex, separated only by a very thin wall.

A lot of the women enjoyed going to Amber's because they were able to see all the men, as they would come and go. They had to come through the salon to get to the barbershop. I think the men enjoyed it, too. They could hear as the women rated them as they walked through.

Andre knocked at my door. I didn't respond to him. Sitting at the vanity, I applied my make-up as if I didn't have a care in the world even though I was nervous as hell. I could be getting a death sentence today. And it's because I fell in love with a man. I placed my life in his hands by trusting him to be what he failed to be. A man. A real man of his word.

"Sade, are you up?" Andre asked from the other side of the locked door.

"I'm up! You don't have to wait for me. I'm driving myself over," I said so he would go away.

I heard his footsteps on the hardwood floor as he walked toward the stairs. As soon as we left the doctors, I would be going to an attorney. We were getting a divorce and the lawyers would decide who got the house. I had my own money and I didn't mind working to support myself. I didn't need a man to take care of me.

When I arrived at the doctor's office, Andre was already in the lobby. He motioned for me to sit next to him but I chose a seat as far away from him as possible. Ten minutes later, we were called into the doctor's office.

A family practice doctor, Judy Spires, was an older white woman. Andre and I had both been seeing her for several years.

"Good morning," she said to the both of us as we sat in front of her huge mahogany desk. She had our folders opened and her glasses were on the bridge of her nose. I tried but I couldn't read her expression. She was playing a poker face.

"Good morning," we both responded nervously.

She closed the folder, sat back in her chair, and removed her glasses. She gave us both a smile. I prayed her smile meant all was well and I didn't have to worry about dying any time soon. I had so many things I wanted to do with my life. I wanted to see my kids graduate from high school and college, get married and raise their children. I wanted to see my grandkids grow up and start their families. I was not ready to die!

"We're fine, right?" Andre said as he nervously wrung his hands together.

Getting straight to the point, she said, "The test results indicate that both of you are HIV positive. I can't say for sure how long because both of you still have strong immune systems." She paused, allowing us a chance to speak.

All I heard was HIV positive. It was as if someone kept stopping and replaying a recording of her voice. HIV positive. HIV positive.

"Are you sure? Can we take the test again?" Andre asked her.

"You can re-test and get a second opinion. I actually recommend it but I'm sure these results are pretty accurate." She handed us a copy of the results. Andre refused to accept his so I took them both.

Tears welled in my eyes. "I'm going to die," I whispered as they streamed down my face.

"Sade, there is no cure but there is medication that enables you to live a full life," she said before adding, "I am so very sorry." So am I! I'm the one who was dying!

"Sade, this is a mistake," Andre said as he stretched his arms around my shoulders, pulling me close into him. "We'll go up to Augusta and get re-tested. Okay?"

Deep sobs racked my insides. "Get off me! This is your fault!" I screamed, as I fled from the office. I could barely breathe. My worst nightmare was now my reality. There was no rewind button. My life was over. All that was left to do was wait for the funeral.

Andre caught up with me in the parking lot before I closed my car door. He used his strength to hold the door open.

Standing between the door and me, "It's a mistake, Sade!" he declared. "It's just a mistake." He really believed his words. He even expected me to believe them. But I didn't live in his make believe world. I lived in the real world where there were consequences for our every action. His actions created the deadly consequences that we both were facing.

"I'm going to my lawyer's office. We're getting a divorce. One of us is leaving the house tonight. If you won't leave, I will." I tried to push him away from my vehicle. His six-four, two-hundred-twenty-pound frame wouldn't budge.

"Sade, don't do that. Please! We can't get a divorce!" he said in a hushed whisper as a couple walked by. Hopefully they wouldn't receive the death sentence I received.

"You expect me to stay married to you?" I asked in dismay. Who was this stranger standing before me? He wasn't the man I married. He looked and sounded like Andre but it couldn't be him!

"Think about what a divorce would do to our careers. We don't need this kind of negative attention. Your book is doing well and my business is doing well, too. Something like this can cause bad press," he pleaded. He then cried, "I don't want my kids to hate me! Please, Sade! Please, let's not get a divorce!"

I thought about our kids. They were all that mattered. I cared less about the book sales and his business. However, I did care about our kids. Even though he was a low life bastard, I didn't want the kids to hate him. Somewhere inside of this monster was the father of my son and daughter.

"We can't sleep in the same room." I heard my words but I couldn't believe I agreed to live his lie.

"This has to stay between us, Sade," he said as he dried his tears with a white handkerchief from his jacket pocket. When I nodded absently, he thanked me and stepped away from the vehicle.

I drove home and wondered how I made it. My mind wasn't on the Atlanta rush hour traffic. All I thought about was Dr. Spires' words. Like a broken record, her words played over in my head: HIV positive.

I wanted to call my sister Nita and tell her what was going on. I needed someone to confide in. I didn't want to live Andre's lie. But, I already promised. If I were to tell Nita, she would kill him and the kids would definitely find out. I rested my head on the steering wheel and cried until

I felt like I was all cried out. I cried until my body shook uncontrollably. I cried until my cell phone rung and my daughter asked, "How's everything going?"

Then I lied and said, "Fine. How are things down there?"

I hated Andre. I hated him for bringing AIDS into our home. I hated him for making me lie to my kids. I hated him for taking me away from our kids. And most of all, I hated him for determining my fate.

Chapter 3

ANDRE AND I MET IN high school. We were both juniors. My family and I moved up from Cordele. My mother had a better job offer in the nursing field that she pursued. Dad, a life long farmer, wasn't happy with the move but agreed to it to support his wife. Nita, my younger sister, and I were scared as can be. We had visited Atlanta but we were country girls who didn't feel like they belonged in the big city.

The first time I saw Andre was in our Chemistry class at Grady High. He had asked me to borrow a pencil and I couldn't stop staring at him. With smooth dark skin and thick eyebrows, his nose was wide, lips were full and his hair was cut low; too fine for words.

When I couldn't stop staring, he cleared his throat and asked again, "Do you have a pencil I can borrow?" I snapped out of my daze and handed him a pencil from my purse. He smiled and thanked me. At that very moment, I was in love.

All the girls wanted Andre. He was the captain of the football team and co-captain of the basketball team. If that wasn't enough of a resume, he was also an honor student. In one package, he had brains, body, and beauty in my eyes.

I wasn't a cheerleader or one of the girls on the auxiliary line. I was a clarinet player and a bookworm. The other girls already had full bosoms and curves. I was straight up and down, and flat all the way around. That's why I was so surprised when Andre asked me out. So were the other girls. They were experienced and I was just a country bumpkin.

We dated for a year before I gave into him and lost my virginity. It was after our Senior Homecoming; we won the game by a touchdown. Mom let me go to the dance without Nita tagging along. Andre's parents were out of town for the weekend and trusted him at home alone since he didn't have any siblings.

The Peters family was wealthy. They had a huge five-bedroom house. Andre's room was as big as our entire house! He was spoiled rotten and I loved him.

Andre and I left the dance early and drove to his house in his Trans Am. I was nervous when we went to his room but after he started kissing me, I relaxed. He kissed me in a way he had never kissed me before. He started at my lips and went down to my neck and then my small breasts. He licked in a circular motion around my navel and then kissed the insides of my thighs. It tickled but not in a way that made me laugh. When he started licking my clitoris, I almost fainted. I had never known that was a part of sex. It felt so good.

I cried when he entered me. He was gentle but I still felt a lot of pain because he had a large penis. I tried not to look at it but it was too big to miss. We didn't use any protection because it was my first time and we didn't believe I could get pregnant. He promised to pull out before he came. I didn't know what that meant but I trusted him. A few minutes after we started having sex I found out what he meant by coming. All of a sudden, he started growling and jerking and making strange faces. I could feel his penis pulsating inside of me before he stopped moving around on top of me.

"What happened?" I asked him when he collapsed on me.

"That's what we guys call busting a nut," he said still panting and out of breath.

"Oh," I had replied.

"I'm going to do it again so you can come," he said as he lifted himself off me.

"How will I know?" I hated to sound so naïve but I really had no clue.

"Some girls say they feel really wet and their muscles start squeezing real hard and real fast on their own," he told me with a smile. I then wonder how many girls he's had sex with before me. "I'm sure you'll know."

He flipped me over on top of him. Straddling him, he placed his hands on my hips to guide me up and down on top of him. I'd never been in that position before but it felt so natural. I don't know how I did it, but I squeezed my muscles around his dick

"Ooh! That's it! That's it!" he moaned. That's when I felt the wet feeling he mentioned.

I moved faster and faster and then I slowed down. Then I screamed, "OH! Andre! Andre!" as my muscles contracted wildly.

He was screaming with me. "Sade! I'm coming!"

He was supposed to pull out but he didn't, said it felt too good. He couldn't lift me up because he didn't want to stop. I didn't want him to stop.

After that night, we made love as often as we could. I would always ride him and squeeze as tightly as I could to show him that I was better than those other girls that he had slept with. In return, he'd always tell me I was the best. Andre could never control himself enough to pull out. We kept coming at the same times. It was the best feeling in the world aside from hearing him say he loved me.

37

Chapter 4

ON GRADUATION NIGHT I, THE class Valedictorian, was two months pregnant. Andre and I had known for about three weeks by that time. We went to the health department. I was scared to tell my parents. We decided we would tell them together the day after graduation. Andre's parents invited my family over to their home for a cookout.

I nearly cried during my speech. Sure, I was emotional about graduation but I didn't like lying to my parents and keeping secrets from them. When Mom noticed me being tired and sleeping more, I convinced her that it was due to the stress of preparing for graduation and college. Having no reason to doubt me, she didn't question me any further.

"I want you to marry me," Andre said after graduation. We were sitting outside my house in his Trans Am listening to Luther Vandross. Maybe Luther's soulful voice made him say that.

"Are you serious?" I asked. I still didn't know what he saw in me when he could have had any girl of his choosing.

"I love you," he said, followed up with a kiss. "Don't you love me?"

"You know I love you. I just don't want you to feel trapped." I told him honestly. I didn't get pregnant on purpose. We agreed that it felt better without rubbers between us.

"Trapped?" he asked, as he shook his head no. "I'm happy. I know we didn't plan this but I always knew you'd be my wife and the mother of my children."

"Yes," I whispered as I bit down nervously on my bottom lip.

"Yes, you'll marry me?" he asked with a big smile on his face.

I nodded.

"We'll make it official tomorrow at the cookout! I'm going to get you a nice ring and then we'll get married right away! We'll get a house in Athens near the campus." He seemed to have everything all worked out so I smiled and agreed.

Our parents did not take the news very well.

"Pregnant?" My father said in dismay.

"How far along are you? Why didn't you tell me?" my mother asked.

"This is probably a trap. Andre you need a pre-nup!" his mother suggested.

"Don't say that, Ella! I think Sade will make Andre a fine wife!" His dad defended on my behalf. He was the only one who didn't hassle us.

"Momma, I'm sorry. I just didn't want to disappoint you and Dad or set a bad example for Nita," I tried to explain.

"Ma, why would you say something like that? Sade is not trying to trap me! We love each other!" Andre yelled at his mom.

"Pregnant?" My father was still in dismay.

"I'm not disappointed. I just want my girls to know that they can always come to me with anything. I won't stop loving you no matter what," Momma cried.

"I'm going to be an auntie," Nita finally realized.

"Pregnant?" repeated the broken record also known as Dad.

"I told you about these fast tailed girls!" Ms. Ella told Andre with her finger in his face. She was so snooty!

"Sade is not like that!" Andre defended.

"She surely is not! I don't appreciate you talking about my child that way, Ella Peters." My mother stood firm with her hands on her hips.

"Pregnant?" I wished someone would've pushed my father in the pool or slapped him.

"Ella! Stop it! Sade is a good girl and Andre is lucky to have her. I'm happy for them," Mr. Jimmy said to his wife. He faced me. "Welcome to the family," he said giving me a fatherly hug.

"I'm sorry," Ms. Ella finally said but it was obvious by her failure to maintain eye contact that she didn't mean it. She didn't think I was good enough for her son. My family was not rich. My mother made good money as a nurse but my father, who was home sick, worked at a factory making average wages. We could never afford a house like theirs. According to Andre, they only have it because when his father's parents were killed in a car wreck there was a big insurance pay off and a lawsuit. Andre's grandparents had been well to do and had passed money down through inheritance. Andre, their only grandson, had a college trust fund set up.

"How are you going to support a wife and a baby?" My mother asked Andre. She wasn't snooty like his mother. She was just concerned about our well-being.

"I'm going to school on a football scholarship. That means I can use the money in my college fund to get us a house and a car. It's a lot of money there to take care of us until I go to the NFL."

Momma shook her head. "You have good intentions but the NFL is a dream; it's not a guarantee." She then turned to me and said, "And what about your education?"

"Mom, I'm not going to let you down. I'll go until the baby is born. When the time is right I'll go back," I assured her.

"Pregnant?"

"Daddy!" Nita screamed as she pulled his arm.

"Baby, take him to the car," Momma said to Nita. To the Peters she said, "Thank you for having us over. I'm sorry to leave so early but this is a lot to take in."

Even though our parents didn't approve, we were both eighteen and we got married on June 15, 1985. We were going to simply go to the courthouse and have a small party with some of our friends. Two days before our scheduled day at the courthouse, Ms. Ella took advantage of the opportunity to make our wedding a social event. She bought me a beautiful gown. My sister Nita was my maid of honor and she wore lavender. Andre's best friend, Ron was his best man. They both wore ivory tuxes. The decorations and flowers were lavender and ivory as well. Everything was beautiful. That day I became Lisa Sade Peters, no longer Sade Taylor.

We moved away right after our wedding. Andre had summer camp. His parents helped us find the perfect three-bedroom house near the campus of UGA. Andre still had his Trans Am and he bought me a brand new Honda Accord. It was blue and just perfect for our small family.

"This is a beautiful house." Momma told me as she helped me decorate my new home. She and I had picked out different shades of blue and ivory.

"I like it, too!" Nita exclaimed. "Y'all should let me come stay here."

"I'm not losing both of my girls." Momma said as she tried to fight back tears.

"Momma! Don't cry because you know we'll all be crying." I said as I placed new dishes in the cabinets.

"I like this house, Sade!" Daddy told me as he helped Andre move in some furniture his parents had given us. His mother was glad to give away a barely used living room suite so she could go buy another new one that would barely be used.

"Thanks, Daddy!" He had finally accepted that I was having a baby.

After dinner, my parents and my sister headed home. Even though we tried not to, Momma, Nita, and me all cried. I was very close to my parents and my sister. We had moved together from Cordele and now I had moved to Athens away from them.

"I'm your family, too." Andre had said trying to calm me down after my parents and Nita had left.

"I know." I sobbed. He was my husband. He would be taking care of me now.

"You don't have to worry about anything, Mrs. Peters. I'll take care of you and that baby boy of ours for life." He said rubbing my rounding belly.

I believed him. He was my husband and the man I loved. I laid my head on his shoulder and allowed myself to feel safe and loved. As long as I had Andre, I would be fine. In less than a week of being married, he had already provided a lovely home for our family and a beautiful car for me to drive. Yes, I believed him. I had no reason to doubt my husband.

Chapter 5

ON JANUARY 1, 1986, I GAVE birth to our twins, Andre Demetrius Peters, Jr. and Andrea Aaliyah Peters. Andre and I had never been happier. Our son looked exactly like him with only my eyes. Andrea also had my eyes and most of my features but like her twin, she had her father's skin color. They were both beautiful.

I went into labor at five a.m. My parents were at the hospital by seven, and three hours later, the twins were born. Andre's parents were vacationing in Europe for the holidays. They had missed the birth of their grandkids.

"They are so beautiful! I can't believe you had twins!" Nita exclaimed.

"I see it skipped a generation," Mom said as she rocked Andrea in her arms. My mother was born a twin. Her identical twin sister, Lisa, died in a car crash at age twenty, with no kids. Her young husband killed himself the day after her funeral. He left a note saying that he didn't want to live without Lisa. I was born a few months after her death, henceforth my first name, Lisa.

"It's going to be hard not seeing them everyday," Mom said. I knew she wanted to be closer to them and me. I would miss her as well. This was all new to me.

"Well, you can come stay on holidays and weekends. We have room at the house," I offered as I watched Nita change A.J. I couldn't believe squeamish Nita was changing a diaper.

"Baby, we don't know how to say this, but we've decided to move back to Cordele after Nita's graduation in May," Dad said gently.

"What? Why didn't anyone tell me?" I cried. We were so close. How could they keep that from me? I needed them as close as possible.

"We just decided on this, Sade," Dad explained. "I miss farming. I just can't deal with this big city living anymore," he said as he put his hands in his pockets.

"What about your job, Mom?" That had been the reason for the move in the first place. Mom was now the head supervisor at Grady Hospital and she made a lot of money. She also loved her job.

Mom shrugged. "I'm going to keep working as a nurse. I'll just be at Crisp Regional now instead of at Grady. Your father's happiness means a lot to me. He really misses the farm."

"It's what I know. I grew up farming. These factory jobs just don't give me the same fulfillment." Dad had a look of longing on his face when he spoke about his farm. "Besides, those people I rented my house and land out to don't know how to run it. I've got to get back home, Sade. Don't you understand?"

I was a grown woman and had just given birth to my own children but I was crying about my parents leaving. "I understand," I said between sniffles. I knew how important the farm was to him.

Andre, who had finally been persuaded to go home and shower, came back into the room. He brought me flowers and a balloon. For the twins he brought two big, teddy bears. One was blue and one was pink. They were both larger than a five-year-old child!

"What's with the long face?" he asked as he kissed my cheek.

"Mom and Dad are moving back home," Nita told him as she handed AJ to Dad.

"And what about you?" I asked. It was her last year in school. I knew she'd be going to college, but she failed to confirm where.

"I'm going to the military," she said proudly. That was news to all of us.

"What?" That was Mom.

"When did you decide this?" That was Dad.

"Nita, I thought you were going to Spellman," I said. That's all she talked about since we moved to Atlanta. She wanted to go to Spellman College and meet a fine brother from Morehouse. Then she would get married and travel the world. She didn't want to have kids.

"The only way I can afford to travel the world is in the military," she told us with her arms folded across her chest. She was very adamant. We could all tell that her mind was made up and there was no changing it. Ms. Nita was almost eighteen. "Besides, I can get an education for free in the military."

I stared at my little sister. She was a year and one week younger than I but a couple inches taller. I had our mother's amber eyes. Nita had our father's dark brown eyes. She didn't have a high yellow complexion like Mom and me. She was a few shades darker than us, but she had our narrow faces, button noses, and pouty lips. She had always been curvier than I. Being pregnant had given me bigger breasts though. Finally.

"I don't like it but you're almost grown now," Dad said as he put an arm around his baby while still holding my son in the other. "I won't stop you."

Mom sighed deeply. She wasn't ready to give in. I decided to speak up for my little sister. I wasn't thrilled about her choice but it was her choice. Besides, she had been supportive of my decision to marry Andre.

"Mom, be proud of her. She's going to get an education in the military. She's going to represent our country. So many people will look up to her." I tried persuading Mom. "Just watch and see. You'll be proud of Nita."

"I think the military is a good choice. If I wasn't playing ball I would've considered it," Andre added.

"You're a man. Little girls don't belong in the Army," Mom said as tears welled up in her eyes.

"Now, Momma. It was always you who told us we could do anything and be anything that we wanted to. You said this is a woman's world just as much as a man's world. How can you say that the Army is not a place for a little girl?" Nita reasoned. She was right. Mom had always taught us to follow our dreams and not worry about chauvinist who felt that women could only perform domestic jobs.

"She got you there, baby! Those are your words," Dad reminded Mom. He handed AJ over to his father and wrapped his long arms around his wife.

"I know what I said. I just…I don't want you so far away, Anita Kimaya." Mom only used our whole names when she was extremely sad, mad, or happy. This time she was extremely sad. We were all shocked when she said, "You better call us all the time. Don't make me come whip your behind in front of Uncle Sam."

Finally, Mom had given in. Nita beamed with pride.

49

Arriving home two days later with our twins, I was shocked to find that Andre decorated both their nurseries. Initially, I only decorated one room for a nursery, choosing yellow and green because we didn't know the sex of the baby. We had wanted to keep it a secret. However, we had no idea that there was another baby hiding in my womb. The doctor had hinted at the possibility based on the weight I had gained but he wasn't sure. The ultrasound showed one baby. The other had been playing a game of Hide and Seek behind its sibling.

Andre, with help from my sneaky mother and sister, had done a great job of decorating the nurseries. AJ's room was decorated with Looney Toon characters such as Bugs Bunny and Daffy Duck. He even had the stuffed animals in his room. There was a crib, a changing table, a dresser, and a rocking recliner. He said the recliner was for him.

In Andrea's room, there was pink and purple everywhere I looked. Her theme was the Care Bears. I knew this had been Nita's idea. She loved the Care Bears. Andrea had a Care Bear in every color in her room. She had all the same accessories that her brother had in his room. Only there was a white glider rocker with a padded cushion, and a matching ottoman, instead of a recliner.

"I love it, Andre!" I told my husband as I stared at the beauty before me. Our kids were so fortunate. Already they were being spoiled rotten and weren't even old enough to enjoy their material gain. All they wanted to do was sleep and eat every few hours.

"Check this out!" Andre said his voice full of excitement. He was so happy to be a father. Most young men ran from the responsibility but my nineteen–year-old husband embraced it. He cried when they were born. He told me God had blessed him twice in ten minutes because Andrea was born ten minutes after her brother, AJ. "Tons of pampers from Mom and Dad!" He pointed at several boxes.

When Andre went back to school, I was left at home during the day with our babies. It was hard juggling two newborn babies but I managed. Andre's mother offered to come and stay with us for a while but I quickly declined her offer. I appreciated her act of kindness but in all honesty, I knew she didn't really like me. She didn't think I was good enough for Andre.

On weekends, my parents and Nita would visit. We wanted to spend as much time together as possible before they moved away and Nita left. She agreed to stay with my family and me until it was time for her to report to duty. She was so excited about basic training and being on her own. I was happy for my sister.

In June, my twins were five months old. My parents moved back to Cordele and a few weeks later, my sister and my helper, reported to Fort Braggs for basic training. Andre was busy with camp. It was just the twins and me once again.

Mom had asked if the kids would be in daycare while I attended college. That's when I broke the news to her. Andre wanted me to put school on hold until he finished and the kids were old enough to go to school. Mom didn't like that one bit.

"What about your dreams, Sade?" she had asked me.

"This is only temporary. My kids come first," I told her.

"You said you'd go back after you had the baby. The babies are five months old. Why do you have to keep putting this off?" Mom worried too much. Dad stood in the corner with his hands in his pockets, while Nita rocked her nephew and niece in the glider. They pretended not to hear the conversation.

"You'll be proud of me, Mom. Just wait and see," I promised her.

She wasn't happy but she didn't push. She called almost every day to check on the twins and me. She tried to persuade me to spend the summer with her and Dad but I knew Andre wouldn't like coming home to an empty house. Every single day he ran into our little cozy home in search of his kids. He would take care of them until they all dozed off in the recliner. I would watch them and thanked God for my family.

Andre and I had a beautiful family. We decided against more kids so I started on birth control. I was blessed to get the gift of a daughter and a son all at once. I never wanted to experience being pregnant again.

Chapter 6

LIFE IN THE PETERS HOUSEHOLD was great. The twins were now healthy three-year-olds. Andre was doing great in school and on the football field. His dream of playing in the NFL was becoming more of an obtainable goal. I was so proud of him. When the weather wasn't too cold, the kids and I attended all of his home games.

I was doing a lot of freelance writing for different magazines. It wasn't exactly glamorous but it allowed me the opportunity to write from home. My family came first and as long as Andre needed and wanted me at home, I was willing to put my dreams off.

My mother visited us frequently. Dad was always busy with the farm and Nita was overseas in Korea. Mom still wasn't happy with the fact that I had not returned to college to complete my education. I assured her that I would enroll as soon as the kids started Pre-K.

Mom was with us the night Andre was hurt during a game. While running a play, he was tackled, falling awkwardly on his right ankle. They first thought it was a bad sprain but x-rays showed that he had a torn ACL. His college football season was over. His dreams of playing in the NFL were also over. He was warned that any further injury to his ankle could leave him crippled for life.

For a while, he moped and pouted. Playing in the NFL had been his long life dream. In one play, his dream was shattered. He still spent time with the kids and me but he also hung out more and more with his teammates on weekends. I had to work hard to meet deadlines because there were times he wasn't there to watch the kids when I needed to work.

"Andre, I need you to watch the kids. This assignment is due Monday!" I complained as I picked up AJ and Andrea from underneath the computer desk. There was no way I could work with them right at my feet pulling at plugs.

"I'm going out! Julian will be here in about ten minutes!" he yelled from our bedroom.

Julian was his best friend. A light-skinned brother, with green eyes and curly, black hair, and a senior at UGA, playing wide receiver for the Bulldogs. I was sure he could have had his pick of girls on campus.

I didn't argue with my husband. I learned from experience that it was senseless to argue with him. We fought many times about this very thing. In the end, he still walked out of the front door, leaving me at home with our two kids.

I put the kids in their playpen and headed to the kitchen to make coffee. I would let them play until they were tired and sleepy, then give them a bath and put them to bed. If I had to, I would stay up all night. Even though my assignment wasn't important to him, it mattered to me.

At two o'clock, I turned off my computer. My assignment was done. I would print it and send it over tomorrow.

I stretched and yawned when I stood. The kids had been asleep since ten o'clock. Andre had not called or come home. Last weekend he stayed out until well after three o'clock in the morning, not offering an explanation as to where he had been. When I asked, he only shrugged and told me he was out with his friends. He assured me that he had been faithful and that he always would be. That had been what I had needed to hear.

ﾉ ﾉ ﾉ ﾉ ﾉ

I decided not to wait up and interrogate him. He was my husband and I trusted him. He was unwinding with his friends. The last thing he needed was for me to nag him and throw accusations. He'd been through enough. His injury had taken a great toll on him.

Even though I did my best to make him happy, he was still hurt over the fact that his NFL dreams were over. He would sometimes cry openly because he felt that he had let us down. I assured him that we still loved him and we'd always be proud of him. We didn't need the NFL to make us a family. We were and always would be a family.

So, I tolerated the late nights. I accepted his lack of support of my career. I did the best I could with our kids. And more importantly, I prayed. I prayed to God to heal my husband's broken heart. Only He could strengthen my husband and our marriage. So, I prayed to Him every night because I knew He would hear my prayer. And He did.

Chapter 7

I FINALLY MADE GOOD ON my promise to my parents. I was now enrolled in college. The kids were in Pre-K. Andre was in his senior year and still participating in team practices and events. And I was now a freshman in college! Things were back on track in our home. I had even completed a novel that was being published. It was just the beginning.

My first novel was loosely based on my life as a wife and young mother. My main character was married to a pro football player. She was the young mother of three who had postponed her dreams in order to support her husband. She ended up having an affair because she felt unappreciated. After all of her sacrifices, she lost her husband. However, she gained a strong relationship with God and went after her dreams. In the end, she was blessed with a second chance with her husband.

"Loved it!" Cindy said over lunch. "It is the best work I've read in awhile."

This was my first meeting with Cindy Brown but she acted as if she'd known me all my life. She was a well-

57

renowned literary agent. A writer gave me her contact information and strongly advised me to call her if I was truly interested in having my book published. I mailed her the manuscript and a month later, she called me to have lunch with her.

Cindy was very talkative. She assured me that she could have my work published by one of the big publishing houses. Even though she smiled a lot, there was sadness in her eyes. I didn't know her well but I knew the look in her eyes. She was lonely.

"Are you okay?" I asked her while we waited on our dessert.

She didn't look up at me. She nodded and said, "Of course. The book is going to be a big success."

"I'm not talking about the book." I reached across the table and placed my hand on top of hers. "I mean are *you* okay."

She looked up and stared at me for a few seconds before saying, "I think my husband is having an affair with his secretary. He's always at his office."

"I'm sorry," I said sincerely as I squeezed her hand.

"Our son is doing well in school but he has no drive. He just...I don't know. I feel like my life is falling apart right before my eyes and there's nothing I can do about it," she sobbed as tears streamed down her tanned cheeks.

"You can always pray about it. I felt alone in my marriage. My husband got hurt and he had a hard time

58

accepting that he wouldn't be able to play football again. He started paying less and less attention to me. But, I didn't give up. I prayed on it."

"And you wrote a wonderful novel," she added as she dried her tears.

I nodded as we both laughed.

"I think we are going to be great friends, Sade."

She was right. We would remain friends until the very end.

Chapter 8

No longer in his slump, Andre and former teammate, Julian Tates, decided to form a sports management agency once Andre graduated. Julian had not been drafted into the NFL but like Andre, he wanted to stay close to the game. Through their agency, they would negotiate contracts for college students going pro. For the first time, in a long time, I saw life in Andre.

Business was slow in the beginning, but he never lost hope. He and Julian had both majored in business, and invested a lot of money and time into the opening of Peters and Tates Sports Agency. I knew they would be successful.

Julian had become a part of our family. Single with no kids, his family lived in New York. Most of his time was spent in our home. To our kids he was Uncle Julian. Andre's parents treated him like a son. My parents treated him like a son-in-law. We all thought he would be perfect for Nita. We could hardly wait for her to come home for Christmas. That's when the two would meet.

I could hardly believe my eyes when I saw my younger sister. After being in Korea for three long years, I couldn't believe so much time had passed, and she was more beautiful than I remembered. Nita also had a very athletic build. I was sure that Julian would fall in love with her at first sight.

"You look amazing!" I complimented my sister after a long embrace.

"So do you!" she said and added, "I see the breasts and hips didn't abandon you." We both laughed as I hugged my parents.

Nita had been home with them for a few days now. They had driven up together in my parent's Denali. As always, my kids came running when they heard my parents' voices.

"Oh my God!" Nita said as she covered her mouth. She had not seen her niece and nephew since they were a year old and trying to walk. Now they were four years old, walking, running, and doing great in school.

"Mommy, who is she?" Andrea asked as she shied away from her aunt.

"This is Auntie Nita. I've told you about her."

"She looks like Grandpa." AJ, who was more outgoing than his twin sister, added. He went right over to Nita and gave her a hug. Andrea soon followed suit.

I had told Nita about Julian in many of my letters to her. She liked high yellow brothers and I was sure that she and Julian would hit it off. He was handsome and she was beautiful. They were both single and had no kids. Our parents already loved him. All we needed was for them to be attracted to each other.

Sparks didn't fly like we had anticipated. They were cordial but the chemistry wasn't there. I think my parents were as disappointed as I was. We had expected them to go out for drinks or for a drive after dinner. Instead, Nita wanted to spend time with the twins and Julian and Andre went out for drinks as soon as Mr. & Mrs. Peters left. They were staying at the Hyatt.

When our parents and the kids turned in, Nita and I were finally alone, relaxing in my bedroom. "Why didn't you like Julian?"

"I like him. He's a nice guy," she answered nonchalantly.

Sipping on hot chocolate, I pressed on. "Okay, but you're not into him?" I muted the sound on the television. *The Cosby Show* could wait.

"To be honest, I think he's gay," my sister said matter-of-factly as she bit into a chocolate chip cookie.

I nearly sprayed hot chocolate everywhere. I had never thought Julian to be gay. He was a pretty boy but that didn't make him gay. He dated. He just had not found the woman that he wanted to spend his life with. I was hoping my sister would be that woman.

"What makes you say that?" I asked Nita after getting over the shock of her blunt statement.

"It's just a vibe I get." Standing, she walked over to the full-length mirror on the opposite side of the room.

"I mean he's way too pretty for me. Besides," she said, smiling as she smoothed her hands over her curvaceous hips, "he wasn't trying to get with me. He has to be gay not to try to accidentally touch my 36-Cs or brush up against my fine ass!" she seductively purred, posing in front of the mirror.

I threw a pillow at her and laughed. She was so vain. Maybe he didn't make a pass at her because she was over confident. That was a turn off for a lot of men. Like Andre, Julian wanted a woman who was not as successful as him. Ms. Nita was very, very independent, never settling for the life that I settled into.

Nita threw the pillow back at me. "You're laughing but if I were you I'd keep an eye on Mr. Julian. He may be trying to steal your man!"

That was absurd. Andre was all man. I wasn't the least bit worried about Julian and Andre being intimate. Sure, they were close but they were best friends. They were business partners. Julian was family.

Even though we all made several attempts to hook the two of them up, it never happened. To appease us, they went out on a couple of dates, but the chemistry wasn't there. Julian assured us that he was attracted to Nita but didn't feel comfortable getting into a long distance relationship. He was in Athens and she was stationed in Virginia.

Nita still believed he was gay, since he never attempted to kiss her or get her into bed. Instead of her thinking of him as a respectful man, she assumed he was gay. With a lot of growing up to do, maybe Nita would be able to appreciate Julian when she was older and more mature.

Julian remained in our lives for the next ten years, until he one day up and sold his half of the business to Andre, and left without so much as a goodbye to the kids or me. They were devastated and wanted to know what had happened to Uncle Julian.

"His parents are sick. He moved back to New York," Andre said with a shrug of his shoulders, offering no further explanation. He moved the company, and us, to Atlanta and lived as if Julian never existed.

We never received a phone call or even a letter from Julian.

Chapter 9

JULIAN TATE. WAS NITA RIGHT about him? Was he gay? Was Julian the one who Andre experimented with in college? Had their friendship been more than just a friendship? So many questions and the only way they were to be answered was if I talked to Andre, no matter how much I loathed looking at him.

Since receiving the test results three months ago, I hadn't spoken one word to Andre. The twins knew we were having problems but didn't push me to talk about it. Andre falsely assured them that he and I would work everything out. He actually believed that he would soon move from the guest room back to our bedroom. I didn't argue, because I knew that day would never come. And, deep down, I'm sure he knew it too.

I agreed to live his lie but I was not going to share a bedroom with him, and fucking him was out of the question. Seeing my husband intimate with a young boy was disgusting and humiliating. And now to add insult to injury, because of him I was HIV positive. My flesh crawled every time he looked at me. Listening to him speak at dinner made me sick to my stomach. As much as I hated the idea of the twins leaving for college, I almost anticipated them being out of the house so I wouldn't have to suffer through dinners with their gay ass father.

I wasn't thinking of Julian until Nita called. Out of the blue she, the ex army brat, asked, "Whatever happened to that pretty boy Julian? Did he ever come out of the closet?"

"We haven't heard from him since he went back to New York. Do you really think he was gay?"

"He was as sweet as sugar! You are lucky he didn't run off with Andre!" she teased as she exploded into laughter.

"I would like to know what happened to him. A.J. and Andrea took it pretty hard when he left. He didn't even say good-bye." I sat down in front of my computer. If he was out there, I could find him on the Internet.

"He probably got mad because Andre wouldn't get with him. That's why he didn't say good-bye. He was mad because you had Andre on lock." If only she knew.

The more Nita spoke, the more I wondered about Julian and the relationship he and my husband shared. Were they lovers? Perhaps Julian did leave because he wanted more than Andre was willing to give. I shivered at the disgusting thought.

"Sade, are you okay?" Nita asked when she noticed I wasn't laughing with her.

"I'm okay. I just got a lot of work I need to do," I lied.

"Okay, Terry McSade," she teased. "Dedicate this one to me."

I hung up with my sister and conducted an Internet search for Julian. Julian Donté Tate was born and raised in Manhattan, New York, one of three sons born to a mother of Island decent and a black father. In the all the years he was a part of our family, I had never met his parents and siblings. Andre went to New York with him on a few occasions and met his family. All I knew about his parents was their names. Sophie and John Tate.

Since Peters and Tate grew into a successful sports agency, I figured Julian was still in the business. I searched until I found an article on him—his obituary—Julian died a month ago. At age forty, he had died in his Manhattan home. His parents and siblings were listed as surviving family. Still he had no wife or kids. I read further hoping that I would find a cause of death. Julian, like many AIDS patients died of pneumonia.

I called Andre's office and Tarylin answered.

"Tarylin, hi, it's Sade."

"Hi! I haven't talked to you in ages! How have you been?" she exclaimed.

It had been quite awhile since we last spoke. I didn't call Andre at work or visit him at the office. If he was having an office party or social function, AJ and Andrea attended. I stayed home.

"I know. I've been swamped," I lied. My whole life had been a damn lie.

"That's what Andre told me. He says you're working on another big novel. I can hardly wait. I love every last one of your books."

We chatted for a few more minutes before she put Andre on. When he answered, I didn't say hello. Instead, I got straight to the point. "Did you know that Julian was dead?"

"Sade?"

"Were you expecting someone else?" I asked rudely.

"No. I'm sorry."

"Answer me. Did you know that Julian was dead?" He had to have known.

He hesitated before sighing deeply and answering, "Yes. His parents called me."

Now I knew something suspicious had gone on between Julian and him. Why else wouldn't he tell me that his long time best friend and former partner died? Julian was like family. There was no reason for Andre to keep that from me. AJ, Andrea and I were as close to Julian as Andre.

I took a deep breath before asking, "Were the two of you lovers?"

"Sade…"

"Just answer me! Were the two of you more than just friends? Is he the one you *experimented* with in college?" I yelled as tears streamed down my face. I knew the answer. The man who had been as close to me as a brother had been screwing my husband right in front of my face. He had come into our home, played uncle to our children. All the while was in love with Andre. How could I have been so naïve?

"I'm not going to discuss this on the phone, Sade. I'll clear my afternoon and come home right after lunch." He hung up before I could protest.

I read the obituary a few times before printing it out. Julian's photo was on the obituary, an old football photo that was taken his senior year at UGA. It was during that time that he and Andre had started spending so much time together. That's when he had become a part of our family.

"Damn you!" I cursed at the photo. "How could you do this to me? I was nothing but a good friend to you. I treated you with respect but all the time you were stabbing me in my fucking back! Damn you, Julian!"

No wonder he had not wanted to pursue a relationship with Nita. He was in a relationship with Andre. Nita knew he was gay. I don't know how but she saw what I refused to see. She warned me to keep my eye on Julian but it was just a joke that we laughed about. I should have paid more attention when she told me she thought he was gay.

69

Damn, how could I have been so stupid? It wasn't as if Andre exuded signs of being a homosexual. But, then again, I'm a country girl, what would I know about the gay lifestyle?

Looking back, I don't remember Julian ever having a serious relationship. We would double date on occasion but he'd always be with a different woman. I never saw the same woman twice. And now that my eyes are wide open, he always acted more like a big brother or a friend to his dates. He didn't act like a lover.

Never had I seen him kiss a woman any place besides on the cheek, hand, or forehead. I had never seen him playfully slap their behinds or squeeze their breasts. I never overheard him and Andre talking about women the way young men do. His focus was always on our family and their business.

I wanted so badly to pick up the phone and call Nita. But, I couldn't. I couldn't chance her knowing the whole story. I hadn't told our parents or the twins what was going on. Quite honestly, I didn't know how to tell them that their mother and father had AIDS. Besides, I was a little ashamed to admit that André had been sleeping with men and I had been too naïve to know. Not to mention what that would do to Andre Jr.

"How are you?" Andre asked when he walked into my home office a little after one in the afternoon.

Sitting on the leather couch holding the print out of Julian's obituary, I held a blank stare. "I thought he was our friend" I finally spoke, my words soft with a hint of pain. "He was like a big brother to me." I looked Andre in the face. "All the time you and him were having sex!" I stood on shaky legs. I closed my eyes. God give me strength, I prayed to myself.

"Let's sit down and talk about this like adults, Sade. I know you're hurt and there are a lot of things I need to tell you. Just sit down and let me talk to you," he replied calmly, careful not to add fuel to an already flaming fire.

"Why couldn't you sit down and talk to me when you realized I wasn't what you wanted? If you had told me everything then I wouldn't be sick with AIDS now!" I was so angry but Andre remained calm. I finally blew off enough steam to calm down.

Seated on the couch, Andre took the obituary out of my hands and held it out in front of him, looking at the photo of the man he loved, at one point, who no doubt gave him AIDS.

"Julian never meant to hurt you, Sade. He wanted me to make a choice between him and you. When I chose you, he left. He went back to New York and we only got together a few times after that. He asked me a few years back to meet him. He said it was very important but I wouldn't go. I wanted that part of my life to be over. My life was all about you, me, and our kids." Andre paused

71

to collect his emotions. It hurt me to the core of my very being to see my husband tearing up at the memories of another lover. A male lover. "When he finally realized I wouldn't meet him, he wrote me a letter claiming that he had AIDS. I thought he was just making it up. He looked fine the last time I saw him. I thought he was using AIDS as a reason to convince me to come to New York, Sade. I didn't know he had really been sick until his parents called me. By that time, it was too late. He was already dead."

"He really did have AIDS, didn't he?"

"Yes. His parents told me he had AIDS," Andre confirmed and I felt my being weaken.

Andre knew his former lover died from AIDS but he failed to tell me. He didn't' tell me that we could be sick. And he'd continued sleeping with other men without telling them. He didn't' even use a condom. Who had he become? All these years, I thought I knew my husband, but in reality, I didn't know him at all.

"Why Andre? Why didn't you tell me?" I couldn't believe his lack of concern for my well-being, for our children's well-being.

He shook his head as he fought back the tears. "I didn't know how. I wanted that part of my life to be over. I chose you over Julian and I tried to bury that part of myself. I didn't want to have anymore desires to be with men."

"But you did," I reminded him as I thought back to the scene in the office three months ago. That part of his life was still very much alive. Homosexuality is not a switch you can turn on and off.

"I know. I tried to control it but I couldn't. He reminded me so much of Julian. I…"

"Were you in love with Julian?" I interrupted.

He shrugged his shoulders. "I don't know. We were close for more than ten years."

"Why didn't you go to the funeral?" I asked curiously.

He turned his attention back to the obituary. "I did. I told the kids I was away on business in Florida, but I went to Manhattan for Julian's funeral. I had to say good-bye to him, Sade. I'm sorry that I lied. I'm sorry about everything."

Andre had hurt me. He had betrayed me. It was because of him that I was now a statistic. I was another African American with AIDS, one more black woman with the disease. One more wife who didn't know her husband was on the down low. For more than ten years, he was in love with Julian. And, for ten years, I lived in the dark.

Why was I feeling sorry for him? He was crying over the man who had aided him in betraying me. They probably made love in their offices. For all I knew they made love in the home we shared in Athens. Maybe even in our bed.

"Where did the AIDS come from?" I had to find out who was responsible.

73

"I don't know. Julian was seeing a few football players, too."

"And you? Were you messing around with clients back then?"

"No. It was just Julian. When he left I didn't touch another man until a few months ago." I didn't believe him. I looked at him long and hard. "I swear it, Sade. There have only been two men that I've had sex with and neither one of them went up in me. I don't play that."

Ignorant ass Andre was back, once again defending his manhood. He was more of a man for not being penetrated, in his opinion.

"Andre, it doesn't matter who went up in who. You had sex with men and now we both have AIDS."

"Sade, I know I've hurt you and I'm sorry. I don't deserve a second chance but I need you. I need you to be my wife again. I'm over that phase in my life. All I want is you. Nobody makes me feel the way you do. Don't you still love me, baby?"

Of course, I still loved him. I didn't like his ass, but I would always love him. Somewhere inside of him was Andre Peters, the boy I fell in love with nineteen years ago. He was my husband and the father of my kids. We've traveled all over the world together. Yes, I loved him. I just didn't know who he is anymore.

"Can you give me a second chance on life? Can you make the AIDS go away?" I asked him.

With his head hung low, "No," he answered.

"The phase of your life that is over is us. I'm out of here as soon as the kids leave," I reminded him as I left him sitting on the couch.

I may always love him but I'm no longer *in love* with him. That phase of my life ended on our anniversary.

Chapter 10

FINALLY, IT WAS THE TWINS' graduation and I was heading to Cordele to spend the summer with my parents. While I was there, I could look for a place of my own. It was time for me to tell the truth about Andre and me. The twins would be leaving for college soon. AJ, like his father, was going to play football at UGA. Andrea wanted to major in medicine at Georgia Tech. Her dream was to become a pediatrician.

"Mom and Dad should have been here by now," Andre said, checking his watch for the tenth time. His parents were running late. They had assured us that they would meet us at the school.

"I'm sure they'll be here any minute," Dad said to Andre.

"Have you tried calling their cell phone again?" My mother asked.

We all—Andre, my parents, Nita and me—were waiting in the auditorium for twenty minutes for Mr. and Mrs. Peters to arrive.

"They're about to start," Nita said when she saw everyone rising out of their seats for the pledge of allegiance.

"They're not answering," Andre said, flipping his phone closed. "Let's just go inside. I'm sure they'll show up soon," He took me by the hand.

I wanted to snatch away and punch him but somehow I was able to refrain. This little façade of his would be over soon enough. After this night, I won't have to pretend with him any longer.

We all cried when Andrea and AJ walked across the stage. They both graduated with honors. I beamed with proud. Graduation night was the beginning of their adult lives. It would also mark a new beginning for me as well.

As graduation came to a close, Andre's cell phone rung. I could tell by his expression that something terrible had happened.

"Are you sure it's them?" he said into the phone as he stared hopelessly at me. "I'm on my way."

"Andre, what's wrong?" I asked as he flipped the phone closed.

"That was the police. I have to go over to Grady Memorial." Tears welled in his eyes and I felt his pain.

"Why?" My mother asked

"It's my parents. They were killed in an accident tonight on the way over here." His voice trembled, as he broke down.

"Oh God, no!" Andrea screamed as she hugged her father.

"I'll drive you all in the Navigator. Nita, you drive Andre's car," Dad ordered.

We drove to the hospital in silence. Sitting beside Andre, I held his hand because I could only imagine the pain he was feeling. He lost both of his parents in one night. When we arrived, I followed Andre into the morgue to ID the bodies. Despite all that was going on in our lives, it wasn't in my heart to let him go through this alone. Even though Mrs. Peters cared nothing for me, I almost lost it when I saw them. They were both badly bruised.

"We found these gifts in the car," the officer said handing Andre two boxes. We both knew they were gifts for the twins.

Andre faced me with a glistening face and red, puffy eyes. "Sade, I know you said you were leaving after the kids graduated, but please, not now. I can't take being alone. I know I messed our lives up but I just need you so much," he pleaded. My heart went out to him.

Maybe he didn't deserve my sympathy but I couldn't be cold. I couldn't walk out and leave him. I would wait until he was strong enough to be alone. My stay would be temporary but I wouldn't leave him in this state.

"I'll stay but nothing changes between us, Andre. And when you're strong again, I'm moving back to Cordele," I said as we walked toward our family.

"Was it them? Are they really gone?" AJ asked his father. His twin sister was still crying hysterically. My father was trying his best to console her.

Andre nodded and reached out to embrace his son. "They're gone, son. But, we're going to get through this. We're a family. As long as I have you three in my life, I know that everything is going to be alright."

"It just doesn't seem right. They didn't even get to see us graduate," AJ said as he fought back the tears.

"But they were thinking of you. The police recovered your graduation gifts." Andre handed one of the boxes to AJ.

"I can't open that, Dad." Our son was devastated.

Andre opened both boxes. In AJ's box was a gold watch. The engraving read: It's your time to shine. We believe in you. In Andrea's box was a gold bracelet. Her engraving read: May you save many lives, Dr. Peters.

Andre broke down again. Was there for him. As much as I hate him, I still loved him. Andrea rushed over, and the four of us cried together. We were still a family.

I didn't go to Cordele for the summer. I was at Andre's side for the funeral. The four of us spent as much time together as possible before the kids left for college. We spent some weeks in Italy. It was like old times. I forgot all about the reality of the problems between Andre and me. It wasn't until we returned home and the kids left that I was reminded of my illness. I had a doctor's appointment.

I was told that my immune system had weakened and I had to start taking medication. My health would never be the same again.

"I'd strongly advise you to stay in Atlanta. The treatment is much better here than down in South Georgia," Dr. Spires advised when I shared my plans of moving back to Cordele.

I didn't argue. Even though I was ready to go home, I obeyed my doctor's orders. I stayed in Atlanta with Andre. He remained in our guest room, and I spent most of my days in the master bedroom. Even though he tried being intimate with me, I declined. I was no longer in love with him. That part of my life had ended two years earlier. I prayed day and night that the rest of my life would last a little longer.

Chapter 11

"HOW'S NUMBER TEN COMING ALONG?" Cindy asked. Three years had passed since my last novel. It seemed that my desire to write was gone. Cindy kept asking about number ten so I finally told her I would give it a try.

I sat in front of the blank screen. It was as empty as I felt inside. My idea for my next novel was not coming to life for me. I envisioned a story about a young mother who was in love with the married man who fathered her little princess. The wife of the married man left when she found out about the affair, but six months later she returned and the young mother was dumped by the man she loved. She then found love in a young man she'd known all her life. The only problem was that she didn't feel she deserved to be loved. It seemed like an excellent storyline but I couldn't get the first sentence on my screen. I couldn't even give it a title.

"I think I've got writer's block," I said to Cindy as I looked through my notebook at the notes I jotted down for the story.

"Well, you know my advice," Cindy began. "The idea we discussed was great but if you're not feeling it…"

I joined in and helped her finish the quote I heard so many times over the years, "Write what's in your heart. There's no better story." She was right. Readers always enjoyed reading emotional stories that seemed believable. An author's work must show that he or she has some type of emotional link to their story even if it is fiction.

"You know best," Cindy said as we both giggled.

We said our goodbyes and I was left to work on at least a title and storyline for my tenth novel.

My previous novels were based on romantic love tales. Even if there was trouble in paradise, the happy couple always worked it out. That had been when Andre and I were happy. The romantic love stories were easy to write. The happy endings were much like the fairytale life I lived with Andre.

Now, the only thing close to my heart was the secret I was hiding from my family and friends. Still no one knew that Andre and I were HIV positive. I avoided my parents for months because of the weight loss. When the twins came home, Andre told them I had ovarian cancer and was going through chemo. Against my better judgment, I went along with the lie.

I felt so bad for lying to them. Andrea cried hysterically. They both wanted to leave school and take care of me. Andre convinced them that he would have a private nurse take the best care of me. He fed my parents and Nita the same lie. Mom, being a nurse, asked detailed questions about the stage of the cancer and the treatments. To my surprise, he was able to answer her questions. Apparently, he had done his homework, and she was satisfied with his answers.

The phone rung as I took out a pen and wrote down new notes. It was time to write from my heart. I was going to write an autobiography. Andre wouldn't agree with my decision but it was my life as well. I wanted to share my story and hopefully save lives. I didn't want other women to suffer my fate.

"Hello?" I answered with a question; I didn't recognize the number on the ID.

"Sade Peters?" A young voice asked.

"May I ask who is calling?" I figured she may be a fan who somehow got my phone number. My last novel had done so well and I received tons of emails about it. My home number was unlisted though and I didn't know how this young woman had come across it.

"You don't know me, but I know your husband." She paused as if she was waiting for me to ask how she knew Andre. When I didn't ask, she continued. "My name is Talia James and I wanted to speak to you about Andre. You know, woman to woman."

I almost laughed. This child sounded to be Andrea and AJ's age. She didn't sound like a *woman* to me.

I gave her the benefit of the doubt though and said, "Okay."

"First of all I know you got cancer and I'm sorry." He had told her the same lie. "But, I'm in love with Andre and he loves me, too. So, since he won't tell you I will." She took a deep breath. "We been seeing each other about six months now. He keeps saying he leaving you but I'm tired of waiting. I know he feel bad about you having cancer and all but I love him and I want him with me."

I couldn't believe what I was hearing. Andre knew we both were HIV positive and here he was sleeping with this young girl. How could the man I once loved be so reckless and cold–hearted to endanger someone else's life? This child had no idea that she had exposed herself to a deadlydisease that can't be cleared up with a visit to the free clinic.

When I didn't' respond she said, "Well, hel-lo!"

"Are you sure you have the right number?" There had to be a mistake.

"Look, I know it's hard for you to believe 'cause y'all been married like almost twenty years but he's not in love with you no more. So, let it go, Sade. You and the twins will be fine." She knew about the twins. Hell, she was calling me by name. There was no mistake. She had the right number. She just didn't know that she had made the mistake of lying down with the wrong man.

A wife should be angry when another woman called to gloat about sleeping with her husband. I could picture this *girl*, smacking on a piece of gum, as if it was the last piece on this earth, with long extensions, twirling a finger around a raggedy strand of fake hair. It wouldn't have surprised me if she wore a pair of those huge loop earrings. And, based on her vocabulary and use of grammar, I doubt she even finished high school. But, despite all of that, she was what I am, a black woman. She deserved to know the truth.

"Did you make him use a condom?"

"A what? What you talking 'bout?" she asked, sounding confused.

Dear God, this child didn't even know what a condom was. I had to break it down in laymen's terms.

"A rubber. Did you make him use a rubber?"

"Sometimes we would but every now and again we wanted that natural feeling. Andre loved going skin to skin," she boasted.

I shook my head. I never thought Andre could be such a bastard. He had already ruined our lives. There was no reason for him to ruin this young girl's life as well. She called my home with intentions of hurting me, but I was afraid she was going to be hurt when all was said and done.

"Don't worry, Sade. Ain't tryin' to get pregnant from Andre. I told him that I won't stop taking my birth control pills 'til we married. I already got two baby daddies who in jail and ain't helpin' me take care they children. Ain't about to get stuck with another baby who daddy ain't gone be 'round. Andre know he gone have to put a ring on this finger before I get knocked up again."

"How old are you, Talia?" The more she talked, the younger she sounded. I was now rubbing my temples because her grammar was giving me a migraine.

"I'm twenty-one years old and no matter what nobody think, I'm old enough to know what I want. What I want is Andre 'cause he love me and my kids."

Twenty-one years old, a year older than my own kids who will turn twenty in January. This girl was just a baby with babies. How could Andre do that to her?

"Talia, have you ever been tested for AIDS?" I asked her. I prayed that she at least knew what that was.

"Have you?" she retorted.

I rubbed the back of my neck. This girl was really working my nerves. "Yes."

"So! What that got to do with me?" She was clueless.

"I don't know how to say this, so, I'll just say it." I took a deep breath. I knew my news would change her whole world, as she knew it. She didn't deserve this. "Andre should have been the one to tell you, but since he didn't I will. We tested positive three years ago."

"Positive for what?" The child asked.

Losing patience with her, I screamed, "We have AIDS! Do you even know what the fuck that is?"

Now she was the one who was quiet. The girl who called me with so much to say now had nothing to say. She was still holding the phone because I heard her breathing. I even heard a gasp as she finally whispered, "Oh my God."

I leaned back in my chair and closed my eyes. I should have felt good about bursting her bubble, but I didn't. Instead, my heart went out to her. No one should have to experience this, let alone a young twenty-one-year-old girl with babies.

"Sade, I'm sorry. I shouldn't have called. Oh, God! Are you sure? Andre don't look sick. He say you just got cancer. Oh, God!"

"Talia, I don't have cancer. Andre lied to you. I have... we both are HIV positive. Andre doesn't look sick yet because he's the carrier."

"I'm sorry," she whispered and I could tell that she was crying. I'm sure she was crying more for herself than she was for me.

"Don't be sorry. Just go and get tested. The sooner you know the sooner you can begin treatment." No matter the circumstances, I wasn't going to leave her in the dark.

"I don't have nobody to go with me. My folks are in Alabama. All I got is my kids and they only four and two. They too young to understand all this." She paused for a second. She then screamed, "I don't wanna die and leave my babies! I'm all they got! I'm all they got!"

I didn't know what to say to her. I wanted to comfort her but what words would make you feel better about the possibility of having AIDS. She's young and she's scared. I felt the same way three years ago. I didn't want to leave my children even though they were older than Talia's kids.

"I probably shouldn't ask you this but will you go with me?" She didn't even know me.

To my surprise I said, "Call me back and let me know the day and time."

I hang up the phone and went out on the patio. The September breeze felt good against my bare arms. It's cool enough for long sleeves but I love feeling the little goose bumps come up on my arms.

"Dear God," I began as I looked up at the partly cloudy sky. I could smell the rain as it neared. "Please have mercy on Talia. I don't want her to suffer my fate. Even though she has sinned against Thee, please be merciful Lord. And God, please give me the strength to be there for her."

I enjoyed the breeze for a few more minutes. When Talia called back and gave me the date and time for her appointment, I sat down at my computer. Now after talking to Talia, there was no more doubt in my mind. I knew for sure what I was going to write. I was going to write my autobiography because I didn't want another woman to be the victim of a down low brother. I was not going to continue to empower Andre by living his lie. I had held on to our secret for three long years. It was time to tell the truth. It was the only way to ease the guilt I felt. If Talia had AIDS, then I was as much to blame as Andre. I should have stood up to him and told the truth. Our kids and my family deserved to know. They deserved the chance to be there for us.

I came up with a name for my novel. There was no better title than, *Blinded by Love.* That's what I was, blinded by the beauty of love. I closed my eyes to everything but the beauty of love. Like Amazing Grace, I was blind but now I see. And now that the blinders were off, I was going to share my story with other black women who may have been living in darkness. I was going to flip the switch and let the light of truth shine.

Smiling, I called Cindy. "I've come up with a story to write." My agent and long time friend was the first person I'd share my secret with.

"Tell me a little bit about it," she said as I imagined her raring back in her executive chair behind her large desk. She obviously had a pen in her hand because I could hear her clicking it.

I told her everything. I didn't leave out a detail, starting with how we met in high school. I told her about Julian who she knew vaguely. However, what she didn't know was that he died from AIDS. I also told her about the young man I caught Andre in the act with in his office on our seventeenth anniversary. She was shocked. When I told her about Talia, she, like me, couldn't believe that the Andre we had once known would be so heartless.

"I'm coming over," she offered but I quickly declined. "Sade, you need me. We've been friends forever. Don't push me away," she argued.

"Cindy, I wish I had told you the truth before because I did have some hard times in the beginning. But now, I've accepted it. I'm fine." She was quiet. "Let me get to work on this story and I'll call you tomorrow."

After finally hanging up with my stubborn friend, I began my autobiography. I know it will change lives.

Chapter 12

I WAS READY FOR ANDRE when he stormed into my office. I knew Talia would call him and confront him. I wouldn't expect anything less. He had put her at risk and I was sure she had questions for him. I was right.

"What the hell did you tell Talia?" he asked without so much as a hello.

Calmly I replied, "I told her the truth." I saved my work and turned to face him. "Andre, how could you do that to her? She's only a year older than our kids! She has two little boys who need her. How could you be so heartless?"

He stared at me as if he despised me for reminding him of our secret. He then walked closer to me. I wasn't worried about him hitting me. He was angry but I knew him better than that.

"Sade, look at me," he demanded. "Do I look sick to you?"

He looked the same but so do a lot of carriers. I shook my head no. "Andre, you look healthy but you and I both know the results…"

"Fuck the results! Doctors are not perfect, Sade! They make mistakes." He was angrier than I had ever seen him. There was also a deep sadness in his eyes as he denied his illness. "I'm not sick!" He shook his head adamantly. "No. I'm not sick!"

"Andre, look at me!" I yelled as I stood up from my chair. I had not told him about my latest doctor visit. But, it was time because I was tired of him living in denial. Maybe my sharing with him would help open his eyes. "I'm dying, Andre! The doctor said I have full-blown AIDS! Look at me!"

We stood face to face. He stared at me taking note of my thinning hair, no longer long, curly, and vibrant. He looked at my once light skin that was now shades darker. He noticed the lesions when I took a Kleenex and wiped my make up away. His eyes then roamed my five-foot-six frame that only carried one-hundred and two pounds. Gone were the hips and the round butt. Then his eyes traveled back to mine. He stared into my sunken eyes that stared back at him from my narrow face. His eyes filled with tears.

"This is what you did to me! This is what you may have done to Talia! Why did you sleep with her knowing that you have AIDS? She's just a child, Andre! How would you feel if someone did that to Andrea?"

As tears fell from his eyes, he shook his head. "It has to be a mistake, Sade. You have cancer. It's not AIDS! I'm not sick!" He was still in denial. Along the way, he started to believe his own lie about me having cancer. I guess it was his way of not taking responsibility for the pain and the ugliness he brought home to me.

Through teary eyes, I studied his profile. He was the carrier. There was no change in his appearance. There were no lesions covering his dark flesh. His dark eyes were still full of life. His six-foot-four frame still carried a healthy two-hundred and twenty pounds. He looked fine but he was HIV positive. He was the reason I was dying.

"You don't know what it's like to wake up every morning and go to bed every night having to swallow a hand full of pills knowing full well that they can't save your life!" I cried as I pushed him away from me when he reached out to embrace my thin body. "Why would you go and sleep with that young girl, Andre? Why?"

He opened his mouth to lie but he quickly changed his mind. He knew there was no reason to deny it. Talia had already told me everything. She had no reason to lie to me. "She reminded me of you, Sade. When I saw her, I saw you and I wanted to have what we once had." I stared at him but I didn't respond. Judging by my earlier conversation with Talia, I couldn't fathom what we would have in common. "It's so hard to be here in this house with the woman I love and not be able to hold you."

"Well, I've got a solution to that problem." I wiped my tears away.

93

He gave me a puzzled look and asked, "What are you talking about?"

"I'm moving back home." When he opened his mouth to protest I continued, "You don't need me any more than I need you. I stayed here because I knew your parents' death was hard for you. I also stayed here because Dr. Spires told me I had better treatment options here than I would have in Cordele."

"And she's right," he argued. The same man who insisted that doctors were not perfect was now siding with one. It didn't matter though. My mind was made up.

"Well, right or wrong I'm going home." I told him as I returned to my chair in front of my computer. "And I'm going to be honest with my family. They should know the truth about what's going on with me."

"Sade…" He wanted to talk me out of it but I was tired of living the lie.

"It's over, Andre. I'm not living your lie anymore," I declared to the man I once loved more than my own life. I cared more for him than I cared about myself. "My children are old enough to know the truth and they deserve to know that I may not be here with them much longer." I choked back the tears as I thought about how sad AJ and Andrea would be when my time on Earth was up. "And I'm going to do what I can to make sure this doesn't continue to happen to other women. I'm writing my autobiography and I'm going to tell the world about men like you."

"Sade, you can't do that. You can't ruin my career like that! Don't you care how this will affect my relationship with AJ and Andrea?" His eyes were pleading with me; begging me not to go public. I abandoned my chair once again and stood toe to toe with him.

"What I care about is my kids and the world knowing the truth. If my book saves one life, I can rest in peace. I'm going to do something to stop the spread of AIDS. I'm not going to sit quietly anymore because you are too ashamed to face the truth." With that said, I left him calling after me. His cries fell on deaf ears.

My mission in life was pleasing him. Well, with what was left of my life, I was going to do whatever I could to make sure not one more woman had to suffer with AIDS and face the final chapter of her life knowing her kids and family would grieve for her once she was gone. It was time to take a stand and that's exactly what I was going to do until I was laying six feet under.

Chapter 13

I MET TALIA THREE DAYS after her phone call. I agreed to meet her at the free clinic. My first reaction when I saw the young girl was shock. She was my height, my former size, and even had my amber eyes, and slim face. She was a few shades darker than me with a wider nose and fuller lips but the resemblance was very obvious. I saw what Andre must have seen.

"Sade?" she asked when I walked over to her. "Dang, we look like we could be sisters!" As I imagined, she had long extensions and wore large hoop earrings. Again, she was smacking the life out of a piece of gum. She looked nervous.

"I was thinking the same thing," I said as I sat next to her.

"I really 'preciate you comin'. I know I done you wrong by messin' 'round with Andre." She was talking me near a migraine. I was so glad when they called her back.

"Come with me?"

When I didn't move, I explained HIPAA to her. The patient confidentiality act wouldn't allow me to go with her. She was reluctant to go without me but I assured her that I would be waiting for her when she returned.

She was back in fifteen minutes. I could tell by her nervous smile that she was scared. "Let me buy you a drink," I offered as we put on our jackets and headed outside. The wind was blowing pretty hard.

Talia checked her watch. "Okay, but I got to hurry. I got to pick my boys up by five-thirty."

We went to a little happy hours bar just down the street. I ordered a gin and tonic and Talia ordered a margarita. The waiter had to check her ID before processing the order.

"I get tired of people treating me like a child," she whined.

"How did you meet Andre?" I asked her after the waiter had returned with our drinks and then disappeared to help other customers.

"He helped me get a job in the cafeteria in his building," she sipped from her frozen drink. "I thought he was so nice. I never woulda thought he was sick 'cause he looked so fine."

"Are you still working?" I took a drink of my own spirits.

She nodded like a little girl. "Yep. But, I wanna find another job 'cause I have to see him every day and it's hard. Sometimes I want to take a knife from the kitchen and just cut his eyes out."

I felt the same way.

"How he get AIDS anyway?" Talia asked.

I cleared my throat. Her question had caught me off guard. I wasn't going to lie to her but I had not anticipated having to explain Andre's sexuality, not today.

"Well, Talia, I found out that Andre had been sleeping with men," I said calmly.

"What!" The girl stood straight up. Other customers eyed her but she didn't care. "You sayin' he gay?"

"Talia, you've got to calm down. You're making a scene," I said as I smiled nervously at the spectators who were now watching our every move. "Sit back down."

She finally stopped huffing and puffing and sat down. "Well, is he gay?"

"He says he's not but I caught him with another man," I explained calmly, praying that she would stay seated this time.

"Lawd have mercy! How come you didn't know your husband was a punk?" I'm sure a lot of people would be asking me that question. Even I wondered.

"How come you didn't know your boyfriend was a punk?" I retorted as I mocked her bad grammar.

She paused for a moment. "I got ya point." She took a long sip from her margarita. I watched as it shrank lower and lower until it was all gone. "So, he's one of them down low brothas I been readin' about. What a damn shame!"

"Did you love him, Talia?" I don't know what made me ask but I found myself wanting to know.

She took a deep breath. "I loved that he treated me good. Nobody else had treated me good before, ya know?" I nodded as if I understood where she was coming from. "But, my best friend, Reggie, told me to be careful 'bout Andre. He told me a man who was willin' to buy my affection came with a cost. I just didn't think the price would be my life."

A sad look replaced the twinkle in her eyes. Her slim face looked even longer. "You'll be fine, Talia. Just pray to God."

"You'll be with me when I get my results, won't ya?"

I finished my drink and motioned for the server to bring the check. I gave her a smile. "I'm sorry, Talia, but I'm leaving first thing in the morning. I'm going back home where my family is. I have a son who is talking about getting married and it's past time for me to be honest with my family about my illness."

I saw tears in her eyes but she was strong enough not to let them fall. "Well, how can I reach ya? I really wanna stay in touch if it's okay."

I gave the young girl my cell phone number and my parents' address. I told her to give me a call as soon as she got her results. Her family that she wasn't very close to was in Alabama. She didn't want them to know she may be sick. They damned her to hell for running off with her boyfriend no sooner than she discovered she was pregnant with her oldest son.

She wasn't ready to hear, "I told you so!" from them. She loved and trusted her neighbor but she wasn't ready to share with him either. He tried to warn her about Andre from the beginning. She wasn't worried that he would say, "I told you so!" She was worried that he would go after Andre and get himself arrested.

I offered her a ride to the daycare facility near her Carver Homes address. Before she got out of the car she said, "I'm sorry 'bout tellin' Andre what you told me. He denied it but something inside me knew you were telling the truth."

"And that's all that matters." I squeezed her hand. "We had a few words but I'm not worried about it. I'm going home. That's all that matters to me."

I watched as she and her two boys hurried to their first floor apartment. All they had were each other and I prayed that she would be around to see them grow up. They waved good-bye to me as they entered their apartment. Two women who sat out front eyed me suspiciously. I heard one shout, "She probably with CPS! The bitch probably tryin' to take that girl chil'ren.' The other woman said, "That's all they do. They think 'cause we po' we don't love our chil'ren. Hell, we love our chil'ren just like they love theirs."

I waved to the two women who looked to be around my age. Both were dressed in bathrobes and slippers. One of the two gave me the middle finger when I waved. They assumed I was one of the bad guys because of the vehicle I drove. Neither of them knew my heart. They had no idea that I was being a friend to the woman who was sleeping with my husband. I wasn't there to take her children away from her. I was praying that God didn't take her away from them.

It was so typical for them to stereotype me. That's what we often did. Often times, men were only perceived gay if they acted feminine. No one looked at the muscular and masculine men and said, "I know he got sugar in his tank." No, it was always the scrawny man with the soft voice who talked with his hands. Even I fell into that trap. I was also one who believed that being gay was not a big part of the black community. Perhaps that had a lot to do with down low brothers living double lives. Some of them may have felt like being gay wasn't a part of their culture. Black people are often not so accepting of gays, especially gay men. Talia's reaction was calling Andre a punk. She wasn't the only one who felt that way.

I raced toward the house. I needed to make a lot of notes about my story. I wasn't going to condemn black men for being on the down low. Somehow I had to get a message across to them that it was okay to be who they were. It just wasn't right to deny who they were and put others at risk. I wanted to save the lives of my sisters and my brothers, one page at a time.

Chapter 14

I DROVE SOUTH ON INTERSTATE 75 with my cruise control on 79 mph. Finally, I was on my way home. I left Andre begging and pleading with me not to leave and not to share our secret. His cries fell upon deaf ears. I was not going to die in vain. I was going to use my voice and my ability to write to reach out to others.

Cars flew by me as I drew nearer to my hometown. I was now in Houston County with less than forty miles of traveling ahead of me. My parents were expecting me but I didn't tell them why I was coming. I wanted to tell them and Nita face to face. I would tell AJ and Andrea on their next trip to Cordele.

Pulling up in front of the old farmhouse, it was a little after eleven o'clock. As soon as I opened my car door I smelled dinner. Momma always had dinner on the table before noon. Daddy would always knock off at that time for lunch. He had farmed for most of his life and it was what he loved most after his family.

"Sade!" Nita exclaimed as she ran toward me. She had moved back to Cordele a few years ago. She spent a lot of time with our parents. "How are you feeling?" She asked when she noticed my way too thin appearance.

"I'm okay," I said as I opened the trunk. Together, we carried my luggage inside.

"Are you visiting or are you moving back in?" Momma asked when she noticed the four suitcases.

"I'm going to stay for awhile if it's okay." I didn't want to say more before Daddy parked his tractor in the backyard. I wanted the both of them to be present when I told them the truth.

"Of course it's okay!" Momma exclaimed as she wrapped her thick arms around my frail body. "Maybe I can put some more meat on your bones. Girl, you as thin as you were in high school! Are you feeling okay?"

"I'm fine Momma. I'm sure your cooking will help me gain some weight." I tried to assure her and myself.

Nita and I both helped Momma finish dinner. Just as we had done as kids, we both ran to the back door when we heard Daddy pulling up on his old tractor. He saw his girls coming and jumped off the tractor running toward us.

"How are my girls?" he asked as he held us close to his heart.

"Fine," we both stated as we vied for his affection.

"Sade, you need a helping of your momma's soul food!" he said when he noticed my size. "You ain't big as a minute, baby!"

We headed inside where Momma already had four plates on the table. She cooked meatloaf, string beans, mashed potatoes and gravy, and steamed carrots. A basket of rolls sat in the middle of the table. The food looked and smelled delicious.

"Go wash up so we can eat!" Momma ordered.

I took my medication before eating. Hopefully it would help me keep my food down. These days I tasted my food more coming up than I did going down. That's why it was so hard for me to maintain a healthy weight. I longed for the days when I was healthy.

"So, what brings my big baby home?" Daddy asked after dinner. Momma was clearing the table while Nita gathered the chilled banana pudding from the fridge. It was my favorite dessert. I prayed that I could enjoy it without getting nauseated.

It was time for me to tell my family, the people I had known all my life, the truth.

When Momma and Nita sat down I announced, "There's something I need to tell all of you. I'm sorry I didn't have the courage to say it sooner."

"What is it?" Nita asked.

105

Momma grabbed Daddy's hand. She could sense that something was terribly wrong when I started sobbing.

"Sade, what's wrong?" Nita asked.

"I don't have cancer." I paused long enough to catch my breath. "I have full blown AIDS." I heard all of them gasp but I couldn't make eye contact with my parents or my sister.

"Oh no!" Nita cried as she wrapped her arms around me. "Why didn't you tell us, Sade? Why didn't you let us be there for you?"

I heard Momma and Daddy crying. They were asking the same questions that Nita asked. Then Daddy asked, "How did this happen? How did you get infected?"

"Andre." Again I had to pause and catch my breath. "Andre had been sleeping with Julian and other men over the years. Julian died not long ago and...Daddy, I didn't know Andre was sleeping with men!"

"I'll kill him!" my father shouted as he slammed a heavy fist down on the table. "I'll kill him!"

Momma tried her best to calm him. "You can't solve this with violence. The best thing we can do is be here for Sade. Let God deal with Andre."

"Nita, you knew," I said as I finally made eye contact with her. "You knew Julian was gay. Why couldn't I see that?"

"Don't go blaming yourself, Sade. You trusted him and Andre because you loved them. It's not your fault that they betrayed you."

I heard her words but something inside of me said I should have known. If Nita knew Julian was gay, I should have known that my own husband was gay. I should have noticed him spending too much time with Julian. I should have questioned him more when Julian up and left without saying a word. Even if I had, would it have changed anything with Andre?

"I'm writing a book," I said after we all calmed down and they promised to be at my side when I talked to the twins. "I'm going to tell my story and hope that other women won't fall victim to this down low episode."

"That's my Sade. No matter how bad things seem, you always find a way to make lemonade out of lemons," Daddy said as he kissed me on the forehead as he had done all my life.

I thought things would change when I told them I had full-blown AIDS. I thought no one would want to touch me or kiss me. I had been wrong. My family still embraced me. They hugged and kissed me. And more importantly, they encouraged me to tell my story. I went to my old room and began typing on my laptop.

Chapter 15

"MOM!" MY SON, THE SPITTING image of his father, yelled as he picked me up in his strong arms. To my surprise, I had managed to gain a few pounds in the two months I had been back at home. Mom's cooking was good for me. My son and daughter didn't stare at me and ask, "Are you okay?"

"Hey, you two!" I exclaimed. I had not seen them in a few months. I had talked to them over the phone and told them I was back in Cordele. I didn't give them the details as to why I had left their father. I'm sure he didn't offer them the truth either.

Andre called at least once a week, begging me to come back home. I refused to entertain the thought. My life with him was over. It was over the moment I saw him with his pants down around his ankles.

I often wondered about the nameless stranger. I never found out who he was or if Andre was ever forthcoming with him about his illness. He probably wasn't a ball player after all. He could have been anyone that Andre picked up off the streets. I would never know.

"Mom, you look good!" Andrea said as she kissed me. "I was so glad to hear that you're done with chemo."

I led them inside out of the chilly November air. It was Thanksgiving and my mother and Nita were preparing a feast. Dad was out back chopping wood for the fireplace.

My kids went in and hugged their grandmother and aunt. I told AJ to go outside and get Daddy. I didn't want to waste another minute being dishonest with them. I lied to my babies for far too long. I had to tell them the truth in order to move forward with my many projects surrounding my novel.

"Hey, Gramps!" Andrea said as she gave my father a big hug.

"Hey, Beautiful!" he said as he squeezed my mini-me in his arms.

"What's this I hear about you getting married, AJ?" I asked my son who still had not shared his news with me. I had heard through my parents that he was thinking about marrying a local girl. I knew her family and knew her to be a very nice girl.

"Calm down, Ma," he said as he wrapped his arms around me. "It's not official. I was thinking of proposing on Christmas Eve and getting married on Easter."

"What about school?" I asked. He was doing very well and I wanted him to finish. "You can't just quit school."

109

"Ma, you know me better than that. Kelita is going to move up to Athens. She is working full time at the bank here and I'm sure she can get a transfer. We'll be able to get an apartment."

"You want a wife or a sugar mama?" my mother teased as she put the last pie in the oven. Nita was setting the table.

"Grandma! You know whether I make it in the NFL or not, I'm going to make mad money after college. Then, my wife won't have to lift a finger." AJ reminded me so much of his father.

It sounded like a good plan. It sounded like a familiar plan. His plans for his life with Kelita reminded me of Andre and me in the beginning. Andre had been blessed with money and neither of us had to work. I prayed that Kelita and AJ's life would have a better ending than my life with Andre.

We enjoyed our dinner and dessert before going into the big family room to relax near the fireplace. I sat between my two kids on the oversized sofa. Momma and Daddy sat across from us on the loveseat. Nita reclined in Daddy's chair.

"There's something I need to tell the both of you." I held each one of their hands in mine. "And I don't want you blaming anyone or harboring any hatred."

"What is it?" Andrea asked as she nervously squeezed my hand tighter.

"It's about Dad isn't it?" AJ asked. "He cheated on you when you were going through chemo didn't he? That's why you left him?" AJ was close but there was so much more to the story.

"Son, your father and I lied about me having cancer. I have full-blown AIDS."

"W-what about D-dad-dy?" Andrea asked her voice low.

"He's HIV positive but he doesn't have full blown AIDS as far as I know." I paused briefly. The look on her face was killing me. "Your father is in denial about this whole thing. That's why he told everyone I had cancer."

"Did it come from him cheating on you with other women?" AJ asked. Before I could answer he was on his feet. "Damn him! How could he do this to you, Ma?"

"AJ! Watch your mouth!" I warned. Momma and Daddy said nothing. They knew he would react this way. Sons are so protective of their mothers. AJ was no different. "Your father is still your father and I don't want either one of you to love him any less or hate him. Understand?"

Neither responded.

I wasn't sure if I should tell them the entire story or not but I decided to be totally honest. My book told the entire story and I wanted them to hear the truth directly from me. "Andre is bi-sexual. He contracted AIDS from having sex with other men."

"My Dad's a punk?" AJ asked as he shook his head in disbelief. "He's a faggot?"

My father spoke up. "Son, I know you're angry, but you were raised better than to refer to people in that way." He didn't approve of the use of such words in his home.

"Well, what else am I suppose to call him, Gramps? He sleeps with other men. What am I suppose to call him?" My son was furious. He was in tears.

"Dad," Momma said. "He's still your father. Keep on calling him Dad."

Andrea was crying softly. She finally asked, "Are you going to die?" We all knew the answer. Even she knew. None of us wanted to answer the question.

"We're all going to die, Andrea," Nita said lightly. "Sade ain't going no where until God calls her home. None of us know when that day will come." She looked me in the eyes and said, "Let's live for today and pray for a better tomorrow."

AJ and Andrea had a hard time accepting all that I had told them. It wasn't easy for them but they took Nita's advice. They found the strength to confront and forgive their father. Along the way, I even forgave him.

My book was released on the same day my son got married. I did many book signings across the country with Momma and Nita by my side. I even made a guest appearance on a few talk shows. I wanted the world to hear me, to see me, and to remember what I stood for. I talked about my life and my battle with AIDS. I talked openly without feeling ashamed. I had AIDS. It didn't have me.

I sent Talia a signed copy of my book. She and I had vowed to stay in touch. We spent a lot of Sunday mornings praying with each other over the phone. I told her that all would be well as long as she kept her hand in God's hands.

My son and his wife came to me on my birthday with great news. In six months, I would be a grandmother. Even though my health had taken a turn for the worse, and not even Momma's soul food was staying down, I prayed to God that I would be around to see my beautiful grandchild born. I also prayed for Andre who confided in me at the Easter wedding, that he, too, was now full blown.

There were days when I was too weak to get out of bed. I didn't have the strength to feed myself. Daddy would hold me up while Momma fed me. He would clean me up when I couldn't keep my food down. Together, Nita and Momma would bathe my thin body despite the many sores. I was in and out of the hospital but they were always by my side encouraging me to pull through one more time.

I was only a few months away from seeing my grandchild born. I was determined not to give up. When I confided in Nita that I was scared of not being around much longer she again said, "Let's live for today, and pray for a better tomorrow."

I didn't give up. My grandchild was born on October 11, 2007. She held my bony finger in her tiny hand. It's the last thing I remembered before slipping into a coma.

God gave me even more than I had asked for. There was only one more thing to ask for. I wanted Him to greet me with open arms and welcome me into His kingdom.

COMING SOON!

Consequences: The Life She Chose
By Linda Herman

CHAPTER 1

Raindrops fell from the grayish blue sky, gently landing on the beautiful rose-colored casket. A spray of white lilies lay on top of the closed casket. Soft cries and audible moans could be heard from those who watched as the casket descended into its awaiting underground tomb. Lisa Sade Peters' earthly life was over. Family and friends stood around, saddened beyond belief at the reality of their loss.

"Momma!" Andrea, her twenty-two-year-old daughter cried out as she reached out towards the casket. AJ, her twin brother, was doing his best to comfort his sister even though he, too, was hurting, wanting to be awaken from the nightmare that they were all having. His mother, their mother, couldn't be dead. It had to be nothing more than a bad dream.

If they weren't hurting badly enough, their father had the nerve to show his face, claiming to grieve for the life that he himself had taken. Their mother was dead simply because of him sleeping with men and then coming home to her. Both looked at him. They watched the shell of a man that had once been their healthy father. Andre now had full-blown AIDS and they knew it was only a matter of time before he, too, would be gone. He deserved to die after taking their mother away. Both AJ and Andrea hated him.

Andre knew it should have been him. He should have been the one being lowered into the ground. He should have been lowered straight to hell for what he had put Sade through. She was the love of his life, a faithful wife and the mother of his children. The children who now eyed him with discontent, their eyes filled with accusation. They hated him. He could see it through their seething eyes. Neither wanted him there. Had it not been for him, their mother would still be alive and well. Andrea and AJ had every right to feel anger and animosity towards their father. After all, he had taken away the one person they loved most in this world, and who loved the unconditionally. He couldn't live with himself.

"Sade!" Andre heard himself cry out, but there was no one there to comfort him. They all hated him. He wanted nothing more than to have Sade in his arms again. He wanted a second chance to make things right. She deserved life.

"My Baby!" Sade's mother yelled, burying her head into her husband's chest. Nita did all she could to comfort her parents, as well as her niece and nephew. She wanted to be the strong one. She had to be. Her big sister was gone now and it was up to her to take care of everyone. But, how? How could she get through this day, let alone, all the empty tomorrows to come? Life without Sade wouldn't be the same. And what hurt more than anything is that Andre, the one who had brought the deadly disease home to Sade, was still alive. Nita wanted to kill him with her bare hands!

As Cindy and Stan stood behind the family, she cried for the loss of her beloved friend, Sade. Sade was more than a client to Cindy; the two had been friends for years. She was there the day Sade slipped into the coma, never to awaken again. Cindy watched her transition peacefully, smiling as she held tightly to the finger of her grandchild. Despite all the sickness and the weight loss, not even the ugliness of AIDS was able to rob Sade of her beauty.

Talia kept her distance from everyone else. Unsure if she belonged, she had to say good-bye to Sade. The woman had befriended her despite her affair with Andre. Sade was by Talia's side when she was tested for HIV. She was the first person Talia called with the results of her test. Sade encouraged her to go back to school and get back into the church. Sade.

Talia looked around. Everyone stood frozen in time. The only movement was the tears that streamed down the many saddened faces. Raindrops were falling hard and heavy now but no one moved. No one wanted to leave Sade behind.

How did it come to be? A woman happily married to the father of her kids, her one and only lover, should not be dead at the young age of thirty-nine. Sade Peters had a heart of gold. She touched the soul of every life that crossed her path. And so many of those souls were there to bid her farewell, a safe journey as she traveled to the Kingdom of God, where a room was prepared for her in her Father's house. However, only one of them could not say good-bye and walk away. Even after the grayish blue sky turned black and the bottom fell out of the sky, Talia James remained at the gravesite looking down at the bottomless pit. She remained there even after the beautiful casket was covered with the earth's dirt.

"There ain't no easy way to say good-bye to you, Sade." Tears fell from Talia's eyes as hard as the heavy rain poured from the sky. She was soaked but she didn't care. All she cared about was being near Sade. "You showed me love when I didn't have no love for myself. You was there for me giving me your love and support when I had brought nothing but more heartache and pain into your life. I didn't deserve you, Sade. I didn't deserve someone as wonderful as you in my life, but you was there. You was there for me and now I don't know how to let you go." Talia dropped to her knees and planted her hands in the muddy dirt. "I'll never forget you. And every day that I live I will live knowing that I should be the one dead. Not you, Sade! I don't deserve the second chance at life that God gave me."

Dropping her head in sadness and shame, Talia made a promise to Sade and herself. "I'm gon' do something with myself. I'll prove my mama and them wrong! I am somebody and I owe it all to you, Sade!" Standing, Talia was finally able to walk away but still she kept looking back, hoping that just maybe Sade would somehow be there behind her.

With her head hanging low, Talia dragged her feet through the thick mud to her rental car. There was a figure standing next to the vehicle. She had thought that she was all alone in the cemetery. To her surprise it was Andre standing next to the silver Malibu watching her and waiting.

"Talia, I just want to—"

"Andre, I'm not here for you," she interrupted. The two had not spoken since the day she confronted him about exposing her to AIDS. Knowing that he was HIV positive, Andre had still had sex with her, unprotected sex. Andre lied to Talia, telling her that his wife, Sade, was sick with cancer. Even after Sade told Talia of their true ailment, Andre continued with his lies. She hated him for having no regard for her life. "I came here to say good-bye to Sade. I don't have a damn thang to say to you!"

Talia pushed past him and opened the door to her car. There was nothing that Andre could say to her that would make her forgive him. His dishonesty was the reason Sade was dead. It was the reason why she would have to retest for HIV every six months for years to come. Yes, the first two test results were negative, but who knew what kind of results she would get when she tested again in three months? She couldn't even live a normal life. Dating was not an option for Talia. The last thing she wanted to do was expose someone else to the disease. She spent all of her time with her boys. But she couldn't talk to them about her fears. They were too young to understand.

Sade was the only person she talked to about HIV. Sade understood and didn't judge her. There was no one else in Talia's life that she trusted the way she had trusted Sade Peters.

"I just want to say that I'm sorry, Talia." As mad as she was at him, she actually turned to face him before slamming the car door in his face. He had never bothered to apologize to her before. She had dismissed the possibility of him ever apologizing. "I know you hate me as much as everyone else does. You have every right to. But, I'm sorry for what I've done to you." Tears rolled down his face. He wasn't the man that she had once been attracted to. His face was now narrow and thin. His once smooth chocolaty skin was now a grayish color. His broad shoulders were razor thin. Even his voice was different. He sounded weaker. "I never meant to...I didn't mean to hurt you or Sade. I just didn't know how to be honest with either of you." He lowered his head. "Or myself for that matter."

Andre didn't know the results of Talia's test results. He was the last person she would call and share that information with. He didn't deserve to know. It was only by the grace of God that she had tested negative so far. If it had been up to Andre, she would be buried next to Sade.

"I agree. You are sorry." That said, Talia slammed her car door, started the engine, and drove away without looking back at Andre. He could rot in hell as far as she was concerned.

Linda R. Herman resides in South Georgia with her husband and their three children. While raising two teens and a two year old, as well as holding down a full-time job as an emergency 911 dispatcher, Linda makes the time to read and write, dabbling in different genres.

Linda anticipates the release of her first novella, *Consequences: When Love is Blind.* Though a work of fiction, the novella will hopefully raise the awareness of women concerning the spread of HIV/AIDS in our community. "It's going to take unity and a lot of faith in God to beat this deadly disease."

Linda's next novella, *Consequences: The Life She Chose* will be released Summer 2008.

A CONVERSATION WTIH LINDA R. HERMAN

Q. *How did you come up with the title Consequences: When Love Is Blind?*

A. The original title was simply *Consequences.* However, I felt more depth was needed and that's when the full title hit me. Sade was surely blinded by her love for Andre and sadly there were consequences.

Q. *How did you come up with the story?*

A. This novella started out as an eleven-page short story. I was constantly hearing about HIV and its rise in the African American community. So, I decided to write a story that would make people stop and think. My book may not change the world but if one life is saved, I'm happy.

Q. *What do you think will be the reaction from some of your readers?*

A. I am sure a lot of readers will initially desire a longer story but when they read the last page they'll know, without a doubt, that the point was executed.

Q. *What do you hope to accomplish by writing Sade's story?*

A. Sade's story was written to raise awareness. I want both women and men to read the story and know that this isn't how life has to be. We can work together to change things.

Q. *Anything you want to tell the readers?*

A. I want to thank my readers for taking a chance on a new author. This is just the beginning for me, and I hope you'll check out my next release, *Consequences: The Life She Chose*. Be blessed and as always, well read.

To learn more about Xpress Yourself Publishing, its titles and diverse roster of authors, visit:

www.xpressyourselfpublishing.org

Printed in the United States
122678LV00005B/64-69/P